"Who are you?" Amanda asked.

Even her voice was different, deeper. If she had hit him square in the jaw with the solid wood, Evan wouldn't have been more stunned.

"Amanda…" he began.

"I—I don't know who you are—" Fear and confusion shook her voice and blurred her green eyes.

Just then a diesel engine drew his attention toward the street, and she gained an opportunity to push the door closed. But then she stopped and stepped over the threshold to stand beside him, trembling in the cold.

A yellow school bus, lights flashing, pulled to the curb. The door opened and a child skipped down the stairs and up the walk.

Evan's knees weakened, and his heart jumped in his chest. The boy had the exact features Evan saw when he looked in the mirror every morning.

He'd not only found his runaway wife. He'd found a son, too. The son he'd never known he had.

Dear Harlequin Intrigue Reader,

We've got an intoxicating lineup crackling with passion and peril that's guaranteed to lure you to Harlequin Intrigue this month!

Danger and desire abound in *As Darkness Fell*—the first of two installments in Joanna Wayne's HIDDEN PASSIONS: Full Moon Madness companion series. In this stark, seductive tale, a rugged detective will go to extreme lengths to safeguard a feisty reporter who is the object of a killer's obsession. Then temptation and terror go hand in hand in *Lone Rider Bodyguard* when Harper Allen launches her brand-new miniseries, MEN OF THE DOUBLE B RANCH.

Will revenge give way to sweet salvation in *Undercover Avenger* by Rita Herron? Find out in the ongoing NIGHTHAWK ISLAND series. If you're searching high and low for a thrilling romantic suspense tale that will also satisfy your craving for adventure—you'll be positively riveted by *Bounty Hunter Ransom* from Kara Lennox's CODE OF THE COBRA.

Just when you thought it was safe to sleep with the lights off…*Guardian of her Heart* by Linda O. Johnston—the latest offering in our BACHELORS AT LARGE promotion—will send shivers down your spine. And don't let down your guard quite yet. Lisa Childs caps off a month of spine-tingling suspense with a gripping thriller about a madman bent on revenge in *Bridal Reconnaissance*. You won't want to miss this unforgettable debut of our new DEAD BOLT promotion.

Here's hoping these smoldering Harlequin Intrigue novels will inspire some romantic dreams of your own this Valentine's Day!

Enjoy,

Denise O'Sullivan
Senior Editor
Harlequin Intrigue

BRIDAL
RECONNAISSANCE
LISA CHILDS

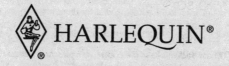

HARLEQUIN®

TORONTO • NEW YORK • LONDON
AMSTERDAM • PARIS • SYDNEY • HAMBURG
STOCKHOLM • ATHENS • TOKYO • MILAN • MADRID
PRAGUE • WARSAW • BUDAPEST • AUCKLAND

ISBN 0-373-22758-2

BRIDAL RECONNAISSANCE

Copyright © 2004 by Lisa Childs-Theeuwes

ABOUT THE AUTHOR

Lisa Childs has been writing since she could first form sentences. At eleven she won her first writing award and was interviewed by the local newspaper. That story's plot revolved around a kidnapping, probably something she wished on any of her six siblings. A Halloween birthday predestined a life of writing intrigue. She enjoys the mix of suspense and romance.

Readers can write to Lisa at P.O. Box 139, Marne, MI 49435 or visit her at her Web site www.lisachilds.com.

Books by Lisa Childs

HARLEQUIN INTRIGUE
664—RETURN OF THE LAWMAN
720—SARAH'S SECRETS
758—BRIDAL RECONNAISSANCE

Don't miss any of our special offers. Write to us at the following address for information on our newest releases.

Harlequin Reader Service
U.S.: 3010 Walden Ave., P.O. Box 1325, Buffalo, NY 14269
Canadian: P.O. Box 609, Fort Erie, Ont. L2A 5X3

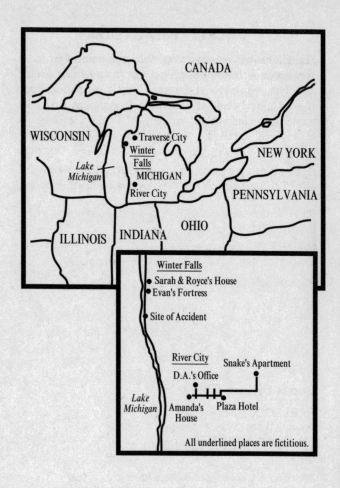

CANADA

WISCONSIN

Traverse City

Winter
Falls

MICHIGAN

*Lake
Michigan*

River City

NEW YORK

PENNSYLVANIA

OHIO

ILLINOIS   INDIANA

Winter Falls

Sarah & Royce's House

Evan's Fortress

Site of Accident

River City   Snake's Apartment

D.A.'s Office

*Lake
Michigan*

Amanda's
House   Plaza Hotel

All underlined places are fictitious.

CAST OF CHARACTERS

Evan Quade—He searches for his missing wife to set her free, but winds up protecting her from a killer.

Amanda Quade—Her memory lost, she has to rely on a powerful stranger to protect her and her son.

Christopher Quade—He's known only his mother, but if a killer's quest for revenge is successful, he'll become an orphan.

William Weering III—Amanda's attacker stole her memory. Now he wants her life.

D.A. Peter Sullivan—His job is to keep Amanda safe, but he fails, either by incompetence or coercion.

Martin "Snake" Timmer—Is his warning meant to prepare Amanda, or panic her into running?

Cynthia Moore—Evan's secretary takes her devotion too far.

Royce Graham—The Tracker reunites the Quade family but can't protect them from a killer's madness, or their unresolved feelings.

To Priscilla Berthiaume, my hardworking, dedicated editor. Thank you for encouraging me to dig deeper into the characters and the story. I couldn't have done it without you! This one is yours!

Chapter One

She'd lost her mind. What other reason did she have for being out at night when she so hated the dark? Of course, she'd been using that excuse for the last six years, ever since she had literally lost her mind. Or at least the part of her mind that held her memories.

Amanda sucked in a deep breath and concentrated on the relaxation exercises the last psychiatrist had taught her. But the extra oxygen in her lungs didn't brighten the dim lights of the parking garage, nor raise the sun in the dark sky outside the concrete barriers. So her pulse raced on.

The stale odors of gasoline and exhaust hung in the cold night air. When Amanda exhaled her deep breath, it lingered as a wisp of fog.

How was it her problem that the bridal shop's deliveryman was down with the flu? She'd suffered through her flu shot in the fall. But when her employment had been threatened by her refusal to fill in, she'd had to leave her sewing machine at home and pack up the wedding gowns to drop back at the shop. Not usually part of her job. She sewed. That was it.

She didn't know how she'd learned this talent, but it was hers. Her one marketable skill.

Or maybe she had more but didn't remember. She clutched her key chain in a tight fist. What did the past matter when she had all she could want now? Well, everything but daylight.

Row J. The scant light reflected off the sign posted on the cement pillar. A few spaces down, her old cargo van stood alone. From under the thin layer of dull white paint, the letters for the name of the previous owner's business bled through. Fawn's Flora. A florist. She smelled the cloying aroma of dried baby's breath lingering in the interior as she fumbled the key into the lock and yanked open the stubborn door.

No reassuring glow from the dome light soothed her frayed nerves. Only darkness reigned inside the van. Dead battery? She glanced down at the illuminated dial of her cheap plastic wristwatch.

Almost bedtime.

She had to tuck Christopher under the covers and pull his cartoon comforter to his little rounded chin. She had to press a kiss into the riotous black curls falling over his forehead. Mrs. Olson had been a sweetie to come over on such short notice and watch her rambunctious boy. But at bedtime he needed his mother.

And Amanda needed him.

She dragged in another deep breath. The burned-out dome light might mean a bad fuse, nothing more. She hopped onto the exposed foam of the threadbare seat and jammed the key in the ignition.

None of the gauges on the dash lit up. The starter

didn't grind as usual, didn't even click. Now she'd have to walk back across the shadowy parking garage to use the bridal shop's phone. Would the repair shop find only a dead battery, or more?

Her sigh shuddered out. If the van needed something major, she had precious little money saved. Long ago she had pawned the expensive watch found on her. All she had left from that forgotten past was the necklace she always wore.

Her trembling fingers lifted to the delicate gold chain, running down it to where the letters began. *A M A N D A* fashioned out of diamonds. Probably worth a fortune, if what she'd gotten for the watch was any indication.

Could she part with her only piece of identification? But what did her name matter when she remembered nothing of the life? All that mattered now was Christopher, and she'd do anything for him. *Anything.*

She lifted her gaze to the rearview mirror to admire the sparkle of diamonds. Perhaps for one of the last times. A shadow sprang up in the cargo area. Before she could open her mouth to scream, a wide hand clamped over it.

The head of a snake tattooed on the back of that hand stared at her in the rearview mirror. "It's okay," a scratchy voice said. "I'm not going to hurt you. Just listen."

Above the hand, her eyes, wide and full of terror, stared back at her, too.

"I've got a warning for you."

Tears threatened, but she blinked them away. She couldn't show any weakness. She hadn't the last time she'd been attacked. That was why she and her son

were alive today. But with her memory, she'd lost
that woman she used to be. Fear paralyzed her.

"That bastard's getting out early. This week."

Hysteria swam in her stomach, nausea rising up the
back of her throat.

"He's gonna hurt you. That's all he talked about.
He knows where you are. And he's gonna hurt you
bad." The hand slid away from her mouth, and she
glimpsed the hairy forearm and the rest of the snake
coiled up the length of it.

"Who are you? And why would he hurt me?" Her
whisper barely made it through trembling lips.

"'Cuz you hurt him. You put him away. Six years.
Not damn long enough. And now he bought his way
into the early-release program."

"Why are you warning me?"

"I got a daughter about your age. I wouldn't want
that bastard touching her. And you're a fighter. You
deserve to know, so you can be ready."

"Thank you."

"Don't. Just get outa town, lady. Reconnect your
battery cable, get your little boy and get outa town."

The cargo door creaked open, the shocks bouncing
back up as he jumped down. Then the slam of the
door rocked the van. Through tear-filled eyes she
glanced into the sideview mirror but only caught the
shadow again.

A warning or a threat? She didn't care. She had to
get out of town. He knew about her little boy. And
he was getting out. Four months before the end of his
too short sentence.

She listened to the news. She had heard the politicians had passed the early-release program to solve

prison overcrowding. Why hadn't she realized that *he* would buy his way into it?

Because there was so little to remember, she never let herself think about the past. Now it intended to pay a vengeful visit.

EVAN QUADE STARED OUT over the city lights reflected in the dark water of the river below his hotel-room window. River City, Michigan.

He liked the simplicity of the name. Amanda would have laughed at it, but then she'd laughed freely. And when she'd left him, the laughter had gone from his life. "I think this is another dead end, Royce," he said, shaking the memory from his mind.

In the mirrored surface of the glass, his friend, Royce, lifted a shoulder and let it drop. Then he held up his free hand as he clutched his cell phone to his ear, whispering into it. Sweet nothings, probably.

The fool was in love. A malady that had struck Evan once and from which he'd never been totally cured. But he'd gotten so sick that he avoided the disease now. At all costs.

And if sometimes loneliness ate at what was left of his soul… Well, his soul was a small price to pay for his sanity. He turned from the window to the table that sat before it. A glossy photo topped the loose documents spread across the cherry-wood surface.

Shimmering blond hair floated loose and wild around her shoulders and beyond. Dazzling white teeth sparkled out of a wide flirtatious smile. Despite the twinkle of naughtiness dancing in her green eyes, he caught the ghost of loneliness looming in the opaque depths.

Amanda had always been lonely, too. Despite her parents' many marriages and a plethora of half and stepsiblings, Amanda had always been alone. Maybe that was why she had thirsted for attention and adventure.

He ran a hand through his hair. In the course of treating his mother's debilitating depression, he'd talked with enough shrinks in the last couple of years that it seemed he'd begun to think like one.

"She's a knockout," his friend said.

Evan glanced up just as Royce tapped his cell phone into his pocket. "Dragged yourself away from your bride?" Evan asked. The ex-FBI agent had married Evan's former business partner less than a year ago.

A goofy smile twisted his friend's mouth. "Barely. And I had to help Jeremy with some homework. Not that he really needed it. Kid's damn smart." Royce's face shone with pride in his stepson.

"Yeah, he's a good kid." Another piece of his soul chipped away as Evan accepted that he'd never have a child of his own. Knowing what he did now, he couldn't.

But six years ago he'd wanted a baby so desperately that his need had stressed his fledgling marriage to the breaking point. If he hadn't fallen so hard so fast for Amanda's gorgeous face and fun spirit, he might have taken the time to discover how incompatible they'd been. The last thing Amanda had wanted was a child, at least his child.

What kind of life did she lead now?

The kind she'd been living when they'd met? Jet-setting? High society?

He'd been working for his father on a business deal to sell warehouse space to a fashion designer. The deal had fallen through, and Amanda, the designer's daughter, had broken the news over a business dinner. But things had not remained business between them for long.

"Evan, did you hear me?"

"What?" Evan shook off the distraction, as thoughts of Amanda often were.

"Jeremy's working on his purple belt. He wants you to run through the kata with him when we get back."

"Gladly, but I'm sure you can teach him what he needs to know."

"I'm not a sensei, Evan. You're ninth degree, man."

"*I'm* not a sensei, Royce." He'd never achieved the degree of control necessary to master the art, the control being over himself. And after what he'd discovered about himself, he doubted he ever would.

He shook off the maudlin thoughts. "She's not in this town, Royce. I've been searching for almost six years. If she'd been living this close to me, I would have found her."

Royce glanced toward the city lights. "River City's just a few hours south of Winter Falls." The small town both men now called home.

"And a few hours north of Chicago, where Amanda and I had lived when she left. But although River City is pretty big and sprawling, it's a world removed in culture and fashion. Amanda had never lived anywhere but a bustling city. Chicago. Milan. Paris. New York."

"But you checked those cities?" Royce asked.

"I checked everywhere. Even morgues."

Evan sighed, remembering the frenzy of his initial search when he'd been convinced she'd needed him. At first the police had suspected his involvement in Amanda's disappearance until they had learned of her stay at her mother's country estate—and discovered what she'd left for him.

Her wedding ring burned against his skin where it dangled on a chain beneath his shirt. Close to his heart, so he would remember her leaving and how much it hurt. So he would never be foolish enough to risk that kind of pain again. "I couldn't find her."

"You've been looking a lot of years…"

Evan understood the inflection in Royce's voice. But even though he'd searched those morgues, he hadn't really believed that she could be dead. Not Amanda.

"You even hired the private investigator that found your biological mother." A search he'd started because of the challenge Amanda had hurled at him when she'd left. Instead of starting a family with him, she'd told him to find the one that had given him up.

His adoptive parents had told him about the private adoption hospital in Winter Falls. He had hired the investigator to find his mother from their records. And he couldn't reveal to Royce, an ex-FBI agent, exactly how that investigator had obtained those records. After the man had found his mother in a sanatorium, Evan had kept him on retainer to search for Amanda. But she hadn't been as easy to find. Years had passed without any leads to her whereabouts.

He admitted, "I never left the search for Amanda

completely to him.'' He'd then fired the guy when his friend and former business partner had married the notorious FBI Tracker.

Royce narrowed his eyes. "You haven't left it completely to me, either."

"She's my wife." Evan rubbed his hands over his face, pressing the heels of his palms against his tired eyes. He'd been looking so long, in the beginning to get her back, and now, to let her go.

Royce sighed. "Maybe if you'd given me more to go on…like the reason she left."

Evan carried his burdens alone, always had, probably always would. Especially now, knowing what he knew, what his mother had revealed to him when she'd recovered. He knew who and *what* his father was…a violent criminal unfit to live in society. "Royce…"

"I know. It's not any of my business."

His friend stared hard at him, trying to crack him with his FBI-agent-interrogation face that Evan had seen before. Then he griped, "Jeez, man, you're one uptight—"

Evan laughed. Royce could always be counted on to speak his mind. The ex-FBI agent thought holding his peace meant carrying a gun. Although they hadn't known each other long, they knew each other well.

"I'm serious, man. You keep everything locked up inside and one day you're going to explode. And it won't be pretty."

Evan's gut clenched, his greatest fear had been spoken aloud. "That's my risk."

One he wouldn't inflict on anyone else, especially not his runaway wife.

Royce sighed as he unwrapped the crinkly paper from a butterscotch, then popped the candy into his mouth. "So you're not going to tell me anything about the past between you and this beauty."

Evan shook his head, not knowing where to start. But knowing that he had to finally accept that it had ended.

The ex-FBI agent crunched on the hard treat. "Tell me one thing. Why are you so anxious to find her now?"

Evan wished he knew. Although he had that gnawing feeling in his gut that she needed him again, he'd been wrong about that before.

He glanced down at the wedding ring banded around the third finger of his left hand where Amanda had slid it almost seven years ago. Then he'd believed they would last forever. But he hadn't known then what he knew now. Amanda had been smart to leave him.

Finally, after a heavy sigh, he answered his friend, "It's time."

Time to truly set her free. And himself.

SHE ONLY HAD A FEW DAYS to pack up over five years' worth of belongings. Amanda tossed toys into an open box, glad that she'd sent Christopher to school that morning despite her initial separation anxiety. Maybe now she'd have everything packed before he got home.

And with that animal in prison for a few more days, Christopher was safe yet. She'd had to convince herself of that before she'd been able to put him on the kindergarten bus. She had to keep as much normalcy in his life as she could right now. When they ran, she'd be turning his little familiar world upside down.

The old doorbell pealed out its disjointed tune, startling a gasp from her lips. Heart hammering, she dragged in a deep breath. *He* wouldn't ring the bell. And as she kept reminding herself, his release wasn't scheduled for three more days.

As she crossed the overcrowded living room, the song rang out again, the notes echoing flatly throughout the small house.

"Who is it?" She hated the quaver of fear that weakened her voice, but the only remedy was safety. She doubted she'd ever feel safe once that animal was out.

"Amanda, it's me."

Relief sighed out as a shaky breath. With trembling fingers she fumbled with the old-fashioned chain lock and threw open the door. "Mr. Sullivan."

The River City district attorney tugged at his wrinkled tie with one hand while he ran his other over his iron-gray hair. "Amanda, I came over today as soon as I could."

"I know." Ever since her attack, Peter Sullivan had been there for her, offering the comfort and guidance of a father since she couldn't remember if she had one of her own.

"The police managed to lift some prints from the inside of your van last night. They're running them now."

"You had the van brought back here, right?" All she wanted to do was load it with all the boxes she'd packed. The prints didn't matter to her. Nothing mattered but safety for her son and herself.

"Amanda, we'll track this guy down—"

"And do what? Arrest him for telling me what you wouldn't? That animal's getting out!"

"I knew you'd get upset—"

"Damn right!" She welcomed the surge of anger sending heat coursing through her veins. Ever since her encounter the night before, she'd been so cold. Now she was hot. "I should have been told he was getting out early."

"Only four months."

"He served less than six years for all the years of my memory he stole." The injustice pressed against her chest, making deep breathing impossible. "He tried to kill me and my unborn child."

The D.A. tugged at his tie again, and frustration wrinkled his already lined brow. "We couldn't prove that. You were only a few months pregnant. He couldn't have known. All we could prove was assault. The witness didn't see everything, and your testimony…"

"He tried to rape me!"

"Amanda, we couldn't—"

"Couldn't prove it. I know. If I hadn't fought…" She would have lost more than her memory.

"You wouldn't be alive. Neither would your son. You know that. I know that, but there wasn't enough evidence to prove it to a jury. Then he and his lawyer kept telling that crazy story that you were a hitchhiker trying to steal his car—that he'd only been defending himself."

She nodded at the appropriate place in their old argument, but frustration and impotent rage rolled through her empty stomach.

"If you hadn't fought, he would have gotten away, Amanda. You took him off the streets for almost six years. You saved a lot of lives of other young women."

She shivered despite the sunshine radiating through her picture window and heating the room. "You're still convinced that I wasn't his first victim?"

"The police could link him to areas where other women disappeared but nothing more. He had no previous record, and there was no evidence to link him to the women who were never found."

Lost. Just as she was. "I disappeared, too."

"Amanda..."

"No, it's true. If not for this necklace, I wouldn't even know my first name. I'll probably never know my last. Whoever I was before he grabbed me, she's gone, too. And after nearly six years and countless shrinks, nobody's been able to find her." She allowed herself to dip into the well of self-pity for just a moment and wonder why nobody had looked for her. No loved ones. Not even the man who'd fathered her baby.

Or had he been some anonymous sperm donor? She had no clue. Nothing but a necklace she would be forced to pawn for traveling money.

Peter Sullivan shook his head. "I can't imagine what you feel like—"

"No, you can't."

He smiled, a weak effort. "Another woman would complain more about the physical scars he left you."

Amanda slid her fingers through her short tresses to the hard ridge of the scar on the back of her scalp. She almost lifted her other hand to the slightly crooked bend of her nose, but what did the physical injuries matter? "No, I'm more upset about what he stole from me. My past. And my courage."

"That's not true. You're very brave in light of your circumstances."

She smiled even though tears of frustration burned behind her eyes. "Very brave for a victim. That's what you mean." She was so sick of being a victim, sick of pity and fear.

"Amanda, you're letting him get to you—"

"No! He won't get to my son or me. We'll be long gone before he's set loose." To her he was a rabid dog. Not William Weering III, not a human being. He was a beast.

Fortunately she didn't remember the attack, but she knew him from the courtroom. From the testimony of witnesses, she knew what he'd done to her and she could guess what he would have done if those witnesses hadn't intervened.

She also knew him from her one visit to him in prison when he'd been properly confined behind bars. She'd screwed up the last of her courage and asked him for her life back. But whatever he'd known of her past, he'd kept locked in his twisted mind behind a cruel grin.

She never intended to see him again.

The D.A. jerked at his tie. "Let me help you find a place to stay."

"No!"

He winced at her shout.

"I'm sorry, but I can't trust anyone now. How did he find me? You made up this last name for me and helped me find this house—"

"You think I sold you out?" Red flooded up from beneath his wilted collar.

"No, not you. But somebody did. His family has money, connections. You told me that. I saw it in court with the high-powered attorney he had. And now he's bought himself an early release."

The D.A. sighed. "The truth is that until we find the guy from last night and confirm the threat, I can't offer you much protection."

"What can you offer me? Can't you keep him behind bars?"

"Not unless we find this guy, Amanda. But I could try for a restraining order."

She swallowed a bitter chuckle. "As if he would abide by it."

He nodded. "You're right. But once he's out, the minute he violates his parole, we'll get him back behind bars."

"Violates parole? And exactly what does that mean?"

The D.A. wore his earnest face. "Missing appointments with his parole officer. Owning a firearm. Associating with known felons."

"Hurting a child? Assaulting a woman? Or murder?" She shuddered. "Once he's out, any parole violation he commits will be against me. And putting him back behind bars will be too late to help me."

The D.A.'s forehead furrowed as he grimaced, reflecting her frustration. He couldn't argue with her and they both knew it. "Amanda, I'm sorry."

"Me, too." On impulse she pressed a kiss against his cheek. Except for her son, she couldn't remember the last time she'd touched anyone.

That was something else she was sure *he'd* stolen from her. Affection, the desire to touch and be touched. By anyone but her son. "Thank you, Mr.—"

"Peter," he corrected her. "How many times have I told you to call me…"

He squeezed her shoulder. "You take care. When are you leaving?"

"Soon." She had more to pack, one gown to finish sewing for the bridal shop, hoping to be part of someone else's memory if only in the fit of a dress. After almost six years of no one finding her, she had accepted that no one searched or Mr. Sullivan would have found a missing person's report on her. He'd kept looking, had kept in contact with other police departments. But then in all these years, she hadn't gotten close to anyone, hadn't ever used this caring man's first name. "I'll miss you, Peter."

He nodded and pulled open the door. "Be careful. And check in with me, so I can tell you when it's safe to come home."

Come home. She had waited years for someone to show up on her doorstep and make that request. No one had come. And she had nowhere to go. But that hadn't stopped her all those years ago and it wouldn't now. She'd run and she'd hide and she'd make a home for her son, even though she doubted she'd ever find one for herself.

FROM THE PASSENGER'S SEAT of Royce's SUV, Evan stared at the small vinyl-sided house. He briefly noted the departure of a gray-haired man who climbed into a nondescript sedan and backed it from the narrow drive.

"A visitor."

"Wasn't there long," Royce pointed out. "Not as long as we've been sitting here."

Evan smiled at the impatience in Royce's tone as he continued to study the plain little house with its white siding and simple black roof. No flash of color. Nothing to distinguish it from the dozens of others lined up the same distance from the curb on the block.

He laughed and shook his head. "There's no way that Amanda's living here."

"You're probably right. This one was a long shot. She uses the name Amanda Smith, really unoriginal. And as you pointed out with your wife's birth certificate and marriage license, *her* real first name isn't Amanda. Hell, Amanda isn't even her middle name."

"Her real first name is Caroline, after her paternal grandmother. But when the inevitable divorce happened, her mother stopped using that name and started calling her Amanda. Probably another husband's mother's name. I don't know. I lost count of my mother-in-law's marriages."

"Her parents haven't heard from her?"

He shrugged. "So they claim. She and her mother rarely spoke. Her mother was always too busy even when Amanda was a child. Neither of her parents was talking to her at the time she took off, so they haven't even looked for her. She'd had a fight with her father, and he had disowned her when she quit working for him. I hadn't even known about it. Probably wouldn't have, but I tracked them down when I couldn't find her. They weren't surprised that she had left me."

As they had gone from relationship to relationship,

they had believed Amanda would do the same. Maybe she had.

"But you were married to this woman?"

Evan ignored the disbelief. "Still am." For now. "At least I never received any divorce papers."

Royce snorted. "Doesn't mean much. Marriage doesn't mean much to some people. You don't have to be separated this many years to file for divorce on grounds of desertion. You could have divorced her pretty easily without ever seeing her again in person, if that's what you'd wanted."

From the corner of his eye, Evan caught his friend's intense stare, but he didn't turn his head. He couldn't comment; it wasn't about his wants anymore. Maybe if he hadn't wanted so much six years ago, she never would have left.

No, she would have left. Leaving was all she knew.

"You're not going to know how wrong I am about your wife living here until you knock on that door." Candy wrappers crinkled in accompaniment to Royce's words.

Evan sighed. "Yes."

He swung open the door and stepped onto the quiet street. "I'll be right back."

"Whatever."

Evan slammed the door and startled some birds from the barren trees. With a hand on his lapel, he pulled his overcoat closer to guard against the brittle cold early-spring air. Despite the bright sunshine, patches of dirty snow stood curbside and the grass was brown and dead.

As dead as he sometimes felt inside…

He might as well get this over. Knock, offer a token

apology for the mistake and continue the search for
Amanda. Purposeful strides carried him across the
street and up the narrow walk to the front door of
Amanda Smith.

He pressed a leather-gloved fingertip against the
bell and winced at the distorted sound echoing behind
the door, which after a few moments opened.

"Mr. Sullivan—" The breathless voice stopped
and green eyes widened behind black horn-rimmed
glasses, the type of reading glasses only available at
a chain drugstore. "Who are you?"

He glanced down her body at the shapeless sweatshirt and baggy sweatpants sagging on her small
frame. Nondescript gray. Amanda had never owned
anything in that color.

He lifted his gaze to her face, peripherally taking
in the shaggy tangle of dark blond framing it. Except
for the slight crook of her small nose, the high cheek-
bones and rounded chin bore a resemblance to the
photo lying on the table in his hotel suite. But that
was all.

She was hardly the glamorous woman who had
worn designer gowns and jetted around the world. But
with one look of her green eyes she still jump-started
his pulse.

"I asked who you are. What do you want?" Fear
trembled in her voice and she stepped back, swinging
the door forward.

Like a pushy salesman, he positioned his foot in
the jamb, so she couldn't shut him out. But if she'd
hit him square in the jaw with the solid wood, he
wouldn't have been more stunned than he was by her
altered appearance.

Even her voice was different, deeper, and her tone diffident, something he never would have expected from his wife. "Amanda?"

"I—I don't know who you are—" Fear and confusion shook her voice and blurred her green eyes.

"Amanda…"

A diesel engine drew his attention toward the street and she gained an opportunity to push the door closed. But then she stopped and stepped over the threshold to stand beside him, trembling in the cold.

A yellow school bus, lights flashing, pulled to the curb across from Royce's SUV. The door opened and a child skipped down the stairs and up the walk.

Evan's knees weakened and his heart jumped in his chest. The boy had curly black hair and dark eyes; the exact features Evan saw when he looked in the mirror every morning.

He'd not only found his runaway wife. He'd found his son, too. The son he'd never known he had.

Chapter Two

Amanda contained her scream of panic by sinking her teeth into the fleshy part of her bottom lip. And she didn't let up the pressure. Another pressure built behind her eyes in a blinding headache. But unfortunately she still had her vision and could still see the devastatingly handsome man who bore such a striking resemblance to her son.

Christopher stopped in front of the stranger, his little mouth falling open as he looked way up at the man. "You're tall."

She swallowed a hysterical giggle over his habit of stating the obvious.

Despite the shock that had stolen the color from the man's face, he found his voice. "And you're not."

"I'm five. How old are you?"

The man chuckled and bent his knees to lower himself closer to the boy's level. Amanda resisted the urge to snatch Christopher into her arms, run into the house and bolt the door behind them. But she couldn't frighten Christopher. Not as she was frightened.

When she'd first opened the door to the stranger,

her pulse had raced, her breaths had grown shallower, what few she'd been able to take...

Who was this man that her body knew even though her mind had no recollection of him? Was he her child's father?

"I'm thirty-five."

Startled by his delayed response, she turned to find his dark stare on her face. Questions raced through the depths of his eyes. He'd come to the wrong person if he wanted any answers.

And he'd come at the wrong time for her to ask any questions of her own. She had no time for the past when she had to secure her future.

"Christopher, what did I tell you about talking to strangers?" The wobble of fear in her voice negated any sternness she'd attempted.

Christopher lifted his head toward her, his dark gaze questioning. "Mom?"

"Go in the house, okay? I'll be there in a minute." She held her breath while he hesitated before the man, then turned to dart around her.

The stranger's gloved hand came up, as if to grab her son, then dropped back to the side of his expensive camel-hair overcoat.

"I don't know who you are, but you better leave!" She backed toward the open door on trembling legs.

"Amanda..."

The tortured sound of her name in his strangled voice stopped her retreat.

"I had no idea..." His deep voice trailed away.

Confusion compounded the headache throbbing behind her eyes. "That's right, you have no idea. And I don't have time to explain anything to you."

His gaze swung around her to the boxes littering the living-room floor. "You're running again? Or still?"

Had she run from this man? Was he someone else she needed to fear? Was that why her heart beat faster in his presence? Fear? She squeezed her eyes shut and lifted a trembling hand to her forehead. "I can't talk to you. You have to leave. Or I'm calling the police."

"And tell them what, Amanda?"

Tell them what? She had no clue who or what this man was to her and her son. If she called, would they remove him? Or her?

Tears of pain from the pounding headache and the burning frustration welled in her eyes. "Please, please, just leave…"

"You think I'm going to just walk away? That was your routine, not mine." Anger blazed in his dark eyes.

"I'll tell the police you're harassing me. I'll call…" The quaver of fear weakened her threat.

"Harassing you? You think this is harassment?"

He stepped so close that the world turned dark as she shivered in his long shadow. His disturbingly familiar scent, rich with wood and leather, teased her senses. But she knew no one who could afford such expensive cologne. And how could she know the cost of the tantalizing fragrance?

Her teeth clanked together. The cold. She'd been standing outside in only her sweats. Had to be the cold that had her trembling uncontrollably.

"Mommy?" called a small voice from within the house.

She jerked back, stumbling over the threshold.

Strong, gloved fingers locked around her upper arm. Holding her upright or just holding her?

"Please…"

She stared up into his dark unrelenting eyes and implored. "Please, go."

The fingers slid from her arm, scorching even through the jersey of her sweatshirt and the leather of his gloves. Branding her. Had she once been his?

No, not a man like this. Too big, too powerful, too much…

"It's not over, Amanda."

His warning hung in the air as she pressed the door closed and leaned against the hard wood, her knees shaking so much they barely supported her.

She closed her eyes against the pain raging inside her head. It was over.

If he returned he would find she'd done just what he accused her of. Ran. But now she ran from two fears, the fear of the animal that had stolen her memory and now the fear of whatever she'd lost with her memory.

EVAN STARED AT THE CLOSED DOOR for several moments, fighting the urge to knock it down and demand answers from this woman who barely resembled the one who had left him nearly six years ago. But that would scare her…and the child.

The child?

He drew in a couple of deep calming breaths. He wasn't in control, not enough to talk to her. Or see the boy again.

He turned toward the street. His friend leaned against the dusty side of his silver Avalanche. In a few long strides Evan crossed the distance between them and grasped the lapels of Royce's sheepskin-lined jean jacket.

Arms straining, he lifted his friend off his heels, gritted his teeth and fought for control of the emotions surging through him. "You knew."

Royce shook his head. "Not that she was your wife. What was the sense in mentioning the kid? Come on, Evan, ease up!"

Evan loosened his hold, letting his friend wrench free. Royce fell back against the side of his vehicle.

"Jeez, man," Royce said, catching his breath. "I knew you ran deeper..."

Still waters? Is that how his friends saw him? Evan fisted his hands at his sides and sought that elusive calmness.

"You going to hit me now?"

Evan caught Royce's glance at his fists and chuckled. "I should, but I don't have time for a street brawl. I need to find out what the hell kind of game my wife is playing. Since she won't tell me, we need to run the plate on that—"

"City vehicle that left here?" Royce passed around the front of the SUV and pulled open the driver's door.

Evan rattled off the license-plate number thanks to his near photographic memory. After the plate flashed through his mind, another image followed. The little boy catapulting down the steps of the school bus.

His son.

EVAN COULDN'T SHUT OUT the ticking of the clock above his head as he listened to Royce and the River

City district attorney swap war stories. After the initial introductions, Evan had remained silent, but it ate at him, bitterness churning with the impatience in his gut.

He leaped to his feet, braced his hands on the D.A.'s messy desk and leaned toward the older man. "We're not here to get acquainted. I need to know what your connection is to Amanda."

"Amanda?"

"Amanda-whatever-she's-calling-herself-now."

"Smith," Royce supplied.

"Amanda Smith?" Peter Sullivan's face was a mask of feigned confusion.

Evan fisted his hands to resist the urge to sweep the paperwork from the D.A.'s desk. "You were at her house just over an hour ago. We saw you. How do you know her and what do you know about her?"

The D.A.'s chair creaked as he leaned back and steepled his fingers over his chest. "If you want any information about Amanda, Mr. Quade, I'm afraid we're going to have to get acquainted first. I know Royce 'The Tracker' Graham. Everybody does. But I need to know you. Who the hell are you?"

"Hutchins's Enterprises, CEO," Royce said.

Evan knew the other man didn't care about his Fortune 500 status. That wasn't the information he sought. From the glint of recognition in Sullivan's blue eyes, Evan knew what he wanted. "I'm her husband and evidently I'm a father, too."

No surprise flashed through the other man's eyes. "You didn't know?"

Evan straightened up and blew out a ragged breath,

reliving the sucker punch he'd gotten when that little boy had scrambled out of the school bus. "No."

"Must have been a helluva shock."

"To say the least."

"So she hadn't told you she was pregnant before she disappeared?"

"No."

"Hmm…"

"What?"

"Well, she was a few months along when she turned up here. And from the remarks she'd made, she'd known before the attack, so I wonder why she hadn't told you yet. Rocky marriage?"

Evan gritted his teeth. "None of your damn business."

"But you never looked for her before?"

"I never stopped."

Sullivan nodded. "She wouldn't have been easy to find, I imagine."

And how much of a part had this man played in keeping her whereabouts unknown? Was his interest in Amanda personal or business? And why did the personal part cause a surge of jealousy to course through Evan's veins?

"I've been working on it for six months," Royce said from where he leaned against the wall.

And during that time the urgency in Evan's stomach had tightened and nearly made him physically ill. Now the clock ticked away the time he had left to figure out what had happened to Amanda and why. She could have packed those boxes into her vehicle by now. She could be leaving River City. And how long would it take him to find her again?

"Did she recognize you?" the D.A. asked.

Evan rubbed a hand over his face, shoving the frustration back. "She pretended not to."

"She didn't pretend anything. Amanda has amnesia and it is very real." He sighed and the lines in his face doubled with his weariness. "Guess the shrinks were wrong. They had suggested that seeing someone important from her past could bring back her lost memory. Unless you weren't that important to her..."

Evan evaded the D.A.'s searching glance, lifting his gaze to the clock on the wall instead. He couldn't argue that he had been important, not in light of how easily she'd left him. To give him time to think... He'd thought all right, he'd thought he couldn't live without her. But her absence had left him no choice.

Royce cleared his throat, probably a nonverbal cue for Evan to give the D.A. some kind of answer. And maybe satisfy Royce's own curiosity.

But Evan had kept his own counsel for too long. "Why does she have amnesia? Was she in a car accident?"

"No."

An uncomfortable moment of silence passed after the man's succinct answer.

Evan thrust his fisted hands into the pockets of his overcoat. He sought his calm center, sought control with deep even breathing. "Are you going to tell me what happened to her?"

The D.A. sighed again. "I don't know if I should. I wish she had recognized you."

"If she had, I wouldn't be here wondering what the hell is going on."

The older man nodded. "That's fair. Okay…a little over five and a half years ago, she was attacked."

The breath trapped in Evan's lungs choked him. "She was what? Was she raped? Oh, my God!" And she'd been pregnant at the time.

The boy's voice echoed in his head. "I'm five." He was fine it seemed. But his mother was not. She'd trembled with fear. Of him? Or every man?

Royce's hand settled on his shoulder, squeezing with empty reassurance.

Sullivan shook his head. "No, thank God! She fought him off. Boy, did she fight him off."

Royce squeezed again. "You gave her that, Evan. You gave her the skills to fight the bastard off."

"What?" the D.A. asked.

"Evan's a black belt in karate. You taught her some moves, right?"

Evan nodded. He'd shown her some moves, but he hadn't taught Amanda how to fight. She'd been born a fighter. Two months early and with no maternal nurturing…she'd been destined to die. But she'd defied all odds then, too.

Evan cleared his throat and clenched his fists tighter. "I want to know everything. What happened?"

Sullivan studied him for a silent moment before he spoke again. "The man, Weering, grabbed her from some other city, we believe. We never found out where. Evidently he kept her in the trunk of his car for some time. Then he pulled over by what he assumed was a deserted section of riverfront."

To rape, kill her and dump the body. To dump Evan's wife and unborn child… Queasiness somersaulted through Evan's stomach. And the name Weering…he didn't recognize it.

"But when he opened that trunk he was unprepared for her assault. She screamed. She fought. She blinded the bastard in one eye."

Royce grunted his satisfaction.

Evan could hardly find his voice over the horror she must have experienced. "But he hurt her, too?"

Sullivan nodded. "Broke her nose and jaw and cracked open her skull."

Evan struggled against the need to slam his fist into a wall. Or into the face of her attacker.

"But she'd screamed so loud before he broke her jaw that help came. Thankfully before she bled to death. And he was caught red-handed."

From Amanda's blood.

Royce's fingers dug into his shoulder again, but Evan could barely feel the pressure through the hatred vibrating in his body. "So he's in prison."

And a good thing, too, because murderous rage pulsed through Evan's blood, begging for vengeance.

"For now," the D.A. admitted.

"What do you mean?"

Red mottled the older man's face. "He's getting out in a few days."

"What!"

"He did his time."

"His sentence was less than six years?"

"We were lucky William Weering III got that much time with the high-powered attorney his rich family bought him." Frustration quivered in the older man's voice. "And then he bought his way into the early-release program. Bastard couldn't even serve out the rest of his sentence.''

''So that's why she's so scared…''

Evan could taste her fear with the metallic flavor of blood from where he'd bitten the side of his tongue, trying to control his anger.

''You probably scared her, too. Christopher bears a strong resemblance to you.''

Evan nodded. ''But her memory…''

''Gone. Blessedly gone in regards to the attack. She remembers nothing of it. She knows nothing from before the moment she woke up in the hospital days after the attack. For Amanda that's when her life began.''

How could memories of their life together haunt his every waking moment and she remembered nothing of it? ''I need to talk to her again.''

''She might be gone already.''

His glance skimmed over the face of the clock again. He should have never left her house until he got these answers from her. But would he have believed it from her? His mistrust may have cost him.

''Do you know where she's going?''

''She wouldn't tell me. She's running scared.''

And Evan was scared of her running.

AMANDA AWOKE TO pounding. The raging headache that had plagued her since the stranger's visit? And following his visit she'd had to deal with Christopher's tantrum. He didn't want to leave his house, his friends, his school… He'd eventually cried himself to sleep on his bedroom floor, where he'd thrown everything out of the boxes she'd packed.

So after forcing herself to finish altering the wedding dress, she'd dropped to the couch for a minute. Just a minute to rest her eyes and will away the pain, so she could resume her frantic packing.

But she opened her eyes to darkness. And her heart clenched with the usual encompassing fear of the dark.

And the pounding continued, interspersed with the sick sound of her half-broken doorbell. Another visitor?

"Who is it?" Her raspy whisper wouldn't carry through the thick wood door, not like the pounding. She cleared her throat and stumbled closer. "Who is it?"

"Evan Quade."

Her pulse skittered over the voice. The name meant nothing to her. "Who?"

"Evan Quade. I was here earlier. We need to talk, Amanda."

She slid her fingers along the chain, making sure it was secure, then edged the door open a crack. Pitching her voice low to not awaken her son, she whispered, "I told you I don't know you. I'll call the police…"

"Call the D.A., Peter Sullivan. He'll tell you to talk to me."

Darkness enveloped him, but she made no move to turn on the porch light. Somehow darkness suited him. In the sliver of moonlight sneaking through the clouds, his dark hair gleamed and his dark eyes glittered.

"I don't…"

A platinum phone flashed between his fingers, and

he pressed buttons. Then he passed the phone through the crack of the door.

When their fingers brushed, she started, nearly dropping the cold metal. Despite the chill air, the warmth of his touch scalded her. "I—"

"Amanda?" The voice emanated from the phone, so she lifted it to her ear. "Amanda, talk to him."

"Mr. Sullivan—Peter?" she asked, double-checking, always double-checking.

"Yes, Amanda. I think you should talk to him."

"Can you guarantee my safety?"

"Physically, yes. Emotionally…"

Emotionally, how fragile was she? Except for her missing memory, she considered herself relatively sane. But Evan Quade looked like the kind of man who could make a woman crazy. She snapped the phone shut and passed it back to him.

"Will you let me in or are we going to talk through the door?"

His deep voice produced a greater shiver along her skin than the cold breeze slipping around him and through the cracked door.

"I don't have time—"

"I'd thought you might already be gone. You were frantic to leave earlier."

She nodded. "I still am, but…"

The dark. She wouldn't be able to travel in the dark, not with frayed nerves, an aching head and the safety of her son her number one priority. She had a couple of days yet. A couple of days before the authorities released an animal.

"Why?"

"You talked to Mr. Sullivan…" She didn't want to speak of the attack, she rarely ever did. But now…

"He told me about the attack and that your assailant is getting out early."

She shivered again, this time from fear.

"Let me inside. You're getting cold talking through an open door."

Automatically she reached for the chain, as if she were used to obeying this man's commands. Who was he? "I don't think that I should."

"I won't hurt you."

"*He* might have said that, too. I don't know. I don't remember."

A ragged breath slipped through the man's lips. "Amanda…"

"No, I don't think you understand. I don't remember *anything*." Frustration bounded back with the pounding against her skull. "You act like you know me. But I don't know that's true. I don't know you. I don't even know *me*."

"Sullivan told me about the amnesia, but I don't believe you've forgotten everything, Amanda." His hand slipped through the crack in the door, his fingers brushing over hers on the chain. Then, exerting just the slightest pressure, he snapped the links and the door swung open. "I don't believe you've forgotten that you're my wife."

She gasped, more from surprise than fear, and stumbled back. He caught her elbows, steadied her, then closed the door behind himself. The house, already small, shrank around his awesome height and lean muscular build. But more imposing than his stature was his aura. Dark, powerful…like his rich scent, teasing her senses and her memory. Her husband? No, she couldn't accept that.

"Where's the boy?" he asked.

"Sleeping." Why did she answer? Why didn't she scream? Run? Where was the fear his action should inspire?

"Good."

She trembled then, her reaction delayed.

"I'm not going to hurt you. I promise."

Physically. But emotionally, she bet he was very capable of hurting her. "Why are you here *now?*" Why hadn't he looked for her years ago if she were really his wife?

"I want to talk to you."

"That's why you're here? In River City? Just to talk to me?" Not to take her home?

"Since I talked to Sullivan."

"And before?" Why had he found her now, after all this time?

"We'll talk about that later, when we have this other situation resolved."

She laughed. She couldn't help it. In her limited memory, *we* had referred to only her and her son. Nobody else. So she'd been the only one solving anything. Alone. And this man, this stranger, thought he could step in and rearrange her life? She wouldn't allow that, even if he *were* her husband.

Something flared in his dark eyes. "There's absolutely no doubt now."

"No doubt about what?" Curiosity prodded her to ask.

"You're Amanda."

"The Amanda you searched for?" The one he claimed was his wife.

He sighed. "For nearly six years."

But whatever had flared in his eyes was gone, leaving them dark and unreadable. No soft emotion accompanied his words. No tears of reunion dampened his eyes. He may have searched for her, but not out of love. She wouldn't delude herself there. She'd already accepted that the only one to ever love her was her son. Her poor heartbroken little boy...

"Something else is wrong," he said, somehow attuned to her moods.

She trembled again, fear of that emotional hurt intensifying. "Christopher doesn't want to leave. Threw the tantrum of all tantrums and cried himself to sleep on his bedroom floor. Very unlike Christopher. Oh, he can be rambunctious, but usually he's too controlled to throw tantrums."

Like a falling star in a dark sky, something flared again in the stranger's eyes. "Controlled?"

"Amazingly so for a five-year-old."

"But he doesn't want to leave?"

"No."

"So why are you?"

"I thought you talked to Mr. Sullivan. You know *he's* getting out."

"But that doesn't mean your life will have to change. You have a new name—"

She choked on another laugh, the bitterness leaving an acidic flavor in her throat. "He knows where I am. Last night I had a visitor. Someone broke into my van and warned me that I'm not safe. He's going to get me when he's released. He wants revenge."

The man, Evan Quade, blew out a ragged breath and some words beneath. "An eye for an eye."

She winced, catching the phrase despite the fact he'd muttered it. "Yes. And with him, undoubtedly more. He has resources. Money behind him. I'm not safe."

She doubted she ever would be again.

Quade straightened, standing impossibly taller. "I have resources, too, Amanda. *I* can protect you."

She laughed, the pitch of it nearing the high brittle tone of hysteria. But she fought against it. "And who will protect me from you?" She gestured at her door and the broken chain dangling beside it.

His handsome face grew tauter, as if he clenched his jaw. "I will. For now."

"Until this situation is resolved? And then you'll tell me what you really want with me?" Not a wife. That much was obvious.

He stepped closer, obliterating the arm's length that had separated them. To focus on his face, she had to tip her head way back. And she had to stay focused, as if magnetically drawn to his dark gaze.

"I don't know why I kept searching all these years, but I did."

She winced, accepting her earlier notion, that he hadn't loved her, as fact. But since he was a stranger to her, why did the knowledge affect her?

"And now you found me? What do you want?" Not her son. She prayed the words in her heart. *Not her son.* Looking into his dark eyes, skimming her gaze over his golden skin left her no doubt that he bore some blood relation to her child. But her husband? Christopher's father? No.

What was his claim and would he stake it? She should have run. The pounding in her head caused the wince and the grimace that twisted her mouth.

His fingers brushed over her upturned chin, up her cheek to her throbbing temple. "Are you okay?"

"No," she admitted. "I'm scared."

Of him. The warmth from his muscular body penetrated through his heavy overcoat and across the few inches that remained between them. But more than inches separated them. Nearly six years and her lost memory. "I don't know you. No matter what you say about being my husband, I don't know you. And I can't believe…"

He sighed and stepped back, his hand falling to his side. "I know. I'm sorry, Amanda, sorry for all that's happened to you."

She didn't want his pity, would have thrown it back in his handsome face, but his voice vibrated with sincerity. "I can help you if you'll let me. Don't leave yet. Talk to the D.A. again. I'm sure Mr. Sullivan's checked me out. He'll verify that I am who I claim to be. Your husband."

He could give her facts, but she wanted feelings. She wanted to know what had been between them emotionally as well as legally. But more than that, she wanted to protect her son and herself.

"I have to leave. I told you—"

"He knows where you live. I'll take you away from here, Amanda. I'll take you—"

"Home?" Heat flooded her face over the longing she'd revealed to this stranger.

"Home? You never really had one."

Her heart ached with the loneliness she never

stopped feeling, not even in the presence of her precious little boy.

"You don't seem surprised. Do you remember?"

She shook her head. "No. No memories. But I have some feelings…"

"Listen to those feelings, Amanda. You'll realize that you do trust me. You'll believe that I can keep you and the boy safe. That I am who I say."

She closed her eyes, shutting out his handsome face, and listened to her heart. Its mad pounding echoed that inside her aching head. Still, she feared him most.

"Amanda…"

"No. I can't trust you." Not anyone. Not ever again. Not now that she knew what evil existed in the world.

"Why not?"

"Why should I?" she countered and opened her eyes to stare into his.

The flicker of light danced in the darkness. "Because I'm your husband."

"No." He kept saying it, but she refused to believe, the implications too many. She stepped back, stumbling over a toy. Strong hands closed over her shoulders, preventing a physical fall. But she suspected an emotional one was inevitable.

"Your name is Amanda Quade."

"No." She bit off the rising hysteria. She couldn't wake Christopher, not now.

"You're my wife," he insisted.

She shook her head and tried to step back again, her stocking feet tripping over the hard plastic truck. A wince was all she allowed herself, no scream of pain. His hands clamped tighter on her shoulders, burning through the jersey material of her sweatshirt.

She couldn't have been married to a man like this. Not her. She was too ordinary. Too fearful. He was too much. "I don't believe you. I wasn't found with a ring on me. Just a watch I already pawned and this necklace."

She dragged the name pendant from beneath the neck of her sweatshirt. Diamonds and sweats. Whoever he'd been married to, she doubted the woman would have worn such a combination.

He chuckled. "That necklace?"

"What? Is it fake?"

"Amanda Quade wouldn't wear a fake."

"I'm not Amanda Quade."

"You're not Amanda Smith, either."

"If I were a married woman, where's my wedding ring?"

His hands slid from her shoulders and he turned away. "I have proof at my house. The marriage license. Pictures. You'll believe me then."

"If I were to leave with you, I'd have to believe you now. And I don't." And she didn't want to. A husband. A father. He'd have a right to her son, probably more right than she had when a judge took into account her psychiatric history because of the amnesia.

"You don't *want* to believe me. You may not remember who you were, but rest assured, you haven't changed that much."

The bitterness in his voice raised bumps along her skin. She didn't believe him, anything he said. Because if he hadn't liked her then, why help her now?

''I don't care about my past.''

The lie burned in her throat, but she swallowed it down. ''I don't have time for the past.''

''You're right that we can't do this now. We need to find this visitor you had.''

''Why?'' She couldn't follow him, couldn't focus on anything with the statements he'd made spinning through her aching mind. Amanda Quade. His wife.

''When he testifies to the threats, we'll be able to block the release of your attacker.''

The D.A. hoped for the same thing, but she'd seen a flaw in his logic, too.

''If you can find him, and that's a strong *if*, how will you convince him to testify? He didn't show me his face. All I saw was a snake tattoo on the back of his hand. And he was big. That's not enough to find him.''

Not since they had found no criminal matches for the prints in her van. The D.A. had called earlier that afternoon with the frustrating news, apparently before he'd met Evan Quade. She hadn't asked him about her strange visitor then, thinking he'd know no more than she had of the mysterious man who resembled her son.

Quade dismissed her concerns. ''We know what prison he was in and whose cell he shared. We can find him.''

''But he won't testify. He seemed scared, too, scared of what Weering can do to him.''

Evan Quade laughed but no amusement softened the deep sound. ''I can do more.''

She shivered and wrapped her arms around her

torso. ''You and I were never married. I can't believe that.''

She, who cowered from shadows, could never have shared a life with a man as dark and powerful as this one.

His long fingers lifted to the silk tie at his neck, pulling the knot then moving down to release the buttons of his black shirt.

''What are you doing?'' Despite the rising hysteria, she kept her voice low, so as not to wake Christopher. She'd already upset her little boy enough.

He paused after the second button, revealing only a patch of golden tanned skin and a tuft of black silky-looking hair. Close links of a gold chain clung to his chest. He tugged at the chain until another object bounced against his chest, clinking against a button and winking in the low light from the lamp.

''I took your mother's advice when I picked this out. She's always equated diamonds with love.''

Looking at the size of the approximately three-carat rock, she guessed that at one time he had loved her a lot, or at least, he wanted her to believe that. And he wanted her to believe they'd been married, that she'd worn this ring.

Which was the lie?

''No.'' She shook her head and tried to step back again, but he caught her, taking her hand and lifting it against his chest. Then he slid the ring, still hooked to the chain, onto the bare third finger of her left hand.

Her hand trembled under the unfamiliar weight of the diamond and against the unfamiliar hardness of his muscular chest. Six years and the head trauma she'd suffered weren't enough for her to have forgotten a man like him. To have forgotten wearing his ring.

She glanced up at the stone and it winked back at her, catching the faint glow from the lamp. And the pain inside her skull intensified.

She closed her eyes but behind them the light from the diamond still flashed, blinding her. Dizziness lightened her head and weakened her knees, and she fell into the arms of the husband she couldn't remember.

Chapter Three

A bead of sweat trickled down between Evan's shoulder blades. The visiting-room door of the minimum-security prison closed behind him, shutting him in with a guard and others who spoke through phones and shatterproof glass to their loved ones. He had no loved ones in prison even though his real father presided there.

In his last argument with Amanda, when he had pressed his wife to start a family, she'd flung at him that what he really wanted was to find his biological one.

And she had challenged him to do that. He had never been able to turn down a challenge. But what he'd found... And what he'd lost...

He'd found a sister, a headstrong challenging sister, and he resented all the years he had not known her. And he'd found an emotionally and mentally broken woman who was his mother. In the course of procuring her psychiatric treatment, his paternity had been revealed. While a teenager his mother had been raped. She had been helping out at a soup kitchen. His father, a homeless ex-con, had taken not only her charity, but her innocence, too.

Every day since he'd learned the truth, he wondered why she hadn't aborted him as her parents had wished. Why torture herself with carrying the child of a man who'd hurt her physically and psychologically? And why love that child enough to give him life, and continue to miss him even after her parents had forced her to give him up?

The guard tapped his shoulder and gestured toward a chair. Evan dragged his feet across the waxed linoleum floor. He wasn't concerned about this man's—this *animal's*—reaction to him. He worried that his reaction to this animal would make him give in to physical violence.

After all, he owed his very existence to a man like this.

He settled onto a vinyl chair that creaked in tired protest of his weight. Through the smeared glass he stared hard at the person across from him.

Pale blond hair hung limply around a face with skin whiter than a corpse. More than prison pallor. Albino maybe. Etched in the pallid skin jagged scars streaked from beneath his eyes. And his eyes…

Evan's stomach pitched with revulsion. One eye was normal but for the extreme paleness of the blue iris. The other eye was scarred and blind; a thick milky film covered the iris, leaving it completely white.

The man held the phone aloft and pointed through the glass at the one on the wall next to Evan. Evan had to uncurl his fingers from a fist to grab the receiver and bring it to his ear.

"Your name's Evan Quade, the guard said. That doesn't mean anything to me."

But something glimmered in that one seeing eye, something like amusement. Did this animal know Evan's name meant nothing to Evan's wife, either, after what he'd put her through?

"It will," Evan responded coldly.

"Don't see how." The man's thin lips twisted into a parody of a grin.

"You're getting out in a couple of days."

"Yeah."

"And when you do, you're leaving town."

"I don't know about that." The man leaned back and drummed his fingers on the Formica surface in front of him.

In a practiced imperceptible gesture, Evan dragged in a deep breath of stale air as he sought his calm center. He would not lose control. "Why not? Is something keeping you in this town?"

"Besides parole, you mean?"

"Yes, because you know parole can be arranged in another city, another state even."

"And you have the connections to know this?" The seeing eye stared intently at Evan.

Evan lifted a shoulder and let it drop in feigned nonchalance, adopting the prisoner's casual attitude. "Yes."

"So you're a powerful man?" In a challenging gesture a pale eyebrow lifted above the blind eye.

"Yes."

The man laughed. "And you're wasting your time with a prisoner who doesn't even know who you are."

"I think you do know who I am. And I'm here because you won't be a prisoner much longer."

"You think I am a threat to someone when I get out?" The twisted grin widened.

"Do I?"

"If you're so powerful, you must be smart, too. Smart enough to know threatening someone could revoke my parole. I would never risk that."

"Not even to settle old scores?"

"Settle old scores? Not even." The scarred lid closed over the blind eye in a wink.

Feeling a surge of anger at the animal's antics, Evan leaned closer, the vinyl creaking beneath his new tense position on the chair. "And now I need you to understand something."

Weering's grin slid into a smirk. "What's that?"

Although bile rose in his throat, Evan forced it down so he could get the words out. "You and I are more alike than you think."

"Really? This is fascinating." The snide tone implied otherwise.

Evan leaned closer yet, so his face was mere inches from the fingerprint-smeared glass. A glance to his side confirmed a visitor pressing her hand against a prisoner's on the other side. "Oh, there are differences. You think you're above the law. I am."

The smirk spread. "I've served my time, man, I don't know what you're talking about. I'm not the one having delusions."

"No delusion. Fact." Evan gritted his teeth, enamel gnashing against enamel. "If someone I care about is threatened, the law won't stop me from protecting her. Nothing will."

"What happened six years ago then?"

His stomach tensed as if he'd taken a roundhouse kick. "I didn't know protection was necessary. Now I do."

Weering lifted a hand in a placating gesture. "Not from me."

"I hope not." Evan waited a moment, then eased back a few inches from the glass. "I called your parents."

Weering's raised hand trembled, and he dropped it into his lap out of Evan's sight. "You what? They're not even in the country. You found them?"

"It was easy. Big spenders leave a trail. They spent a lot on your lawyers, too. Even spent some money to guarantee you'd be part of the early-release program. I traced some of their political contributions."

For a moment, William seemed unsettled, but then his mask of indifference returned. "So? Parents getting their only child out early, what's wrong with that?"

Evan laughed out his derision. "Nothing, if they were loving parents. But they're not. In fact, they seem to fear you. Odd that they left the country just prior to your release…"

Because of that—and the fearful tone of Mrs. Weering's voice—Evan was tempted to whisk Amanda and Christopher from the country, too. If this man was so evil his own parents feared him…

Evan had failed Amanda before. He hadn't protected her from this madman once. Although he'd give his life if necessary, would it be enough to keep her safe?

"So? My parents don't love me. They just stick by me out of duty." He grated the words into the phone.

Evan narrowed his eyes in anticipation of a wrong move from the prisoner. He'd found the switch to turn off the man's nonchalance. "Or blackmail." Evan figured Weering had something on his parents, something that allowed him to control them even though they feared him.

"Some parents don't love their children, whether they had them or adopted them," Weering continued. "Children are a status symbol and sometimes worse. You know that."

Evan's muscles tensed as he sat poised for the man's counterattack. "Do I?"

"And earlier when you said we're similar, there was something you forgot to mention." The smirk slid back into place now, but the slight flush on the pale skin suggested his loss of control.

"What?"

"We've got the same kind of genes. So maybe you shouldn't worry about protecting your wife and kid from me, but from yourself!"

Evan's control almost slipped from the chain he'd padlocked around it. In his mind he could see himself vaulting out of the chair and through the glass barrier. He'd broken bricks with his bare hands. What challenge would shatterproof glass pose?

None. The challenge was in keeping his temper tethered. Especially now, since he was aware of those genes.

How in the hell did the man know about his father—something so few others knew? Evan managed a careless shrug. "I thought you didn't know who I was?"

Weering shook his head, disappointment stealing his smirk away. "Who said I did?"

"And all this time you've known who Amanda is, but you've never told anyone. Kept her identification as a trophy, did you?"

The prisoner shrugged his shoulders. "I think we've said all there is to say. You've made your threats. We're through." He started to lift the receiver from his ear.

"No!"

The seeing eye widened, as the man evidently anticipated an outburst and relished it.

Evan forced a grin. "I need to clarify what I said earlier. And since you really know more about me than you admitted at first, you'll know it's true. I won't just protect what's mine. I'll take care of whoever's threatening them. I'll eliminate that threat."

The convict snorted. "By using the law. So you're rich. You have connections with politicians and cops."

"Yes, I do. But I wouldn't rely on my friends. I'd take care of the problem with my own hands." On that last note, he replaced the receiver, severing the connection.

Weering's mouth moved as if he were laughing, but the soundproof glass spared Evan from listening to the sick notes of a madman's laughter.

AMANDA HEFTED ANOTHER box through the cargo doors of her van, settling the weighted-down cardboard onto the rusted floor. A glance over her shoulder confirmed that the silver SUV was still parked across the street. The man behind the wheel didn't even pretend that he wasn't watching her. She didn't know him, but she knew who had sent him.

Her *husband*.

Could it be true?

When she straightened away from the van, the chilly spring wind whipped around the open doors and stole her breath. Just as he'd stolen her breath last night. When she'd fainted into his arms.

Heat rushed up, chasing the windburn away to leave another kind of burn. Embarrassment. Had she really fallen into his arms like some silent movie starlet?

The headache. Ever since the attack, she'd fallen victim to debilitating migraines. She'd had one before seeing that ring. Her fainting spell had had nothing to do with the glittering diamond.

When she'd awakened on the couch, she had almost convinced herself that she'd dreamed the whole thing, until he had returned to press a cold cloth against her forehead. He'd knelt beside her, and for once she'd recognized the emotion in his dark eyes. Concern. For her.

That had staggered her as much as the ring, which had disappeared inside his silk shirt to nestle against his muscular chest. But he hadn't retightened the tie, so the thin chain gleamed in the lamplight as a reminder of what she'd seen—what had graced her hand. A perfect fit.

Somehow she figured Cinderella would have preferred that magnificent diamond over the shoe. But she wasn't Cinderella, and almost six years ago, she'd learned fairy tales bore no resemblance to reality except for the element of evil. Evil was the only reality Amanda knew. And she doubted it would ever be conquered.

All she could do was run.

"Amanda, let me help you." The words he'd whispered as he'd knelt beside her last night washed over her again. "Let me help you."

Panic had crashed over her next, like the foam following a lapping wave. Frenzied. "Please, leave. Leave before Christopher wakes up. I can't deal with this now...with you. Please, just go."

She had been stunned again when he'd complied, pausing only at the door to glance back at her with an unreadable expression in those dark eyes. About ten minutes later a locksmith had arrived to replace her broken chain with a new dead bolt.

Evan Quade had left twice when she'd pleaded. She didn't count on her luck holding out a third time. When she stepped outside with another box, she automatically glanced to her shadow across the road. And she saw another shadow, a tall dark one.

Evan.

Behind the SUV, a racy red sports car idled, puffs of exhaust hanging in the cold air. Suspended. Like her. The weight of the box dragged at her arms and a tingling pain shot from her wrists to an unreachable pressure point between her shoulder blades.

A curse drifted across to her before the scrape of his shoes on the asphalt as he rushed across the street and wrestled the box from her arms. "You're going to hurt yourself."

She swallowed a hysterical giggle. "Why didn't you have your friend help me then?"

"Royce?" He chuckled, the deep rumble warming her. "He's no gentleman."

"I gathered that." She arched, but the stubborn ache remained.

"He was busy on the phone. And once you had everything packed up, what would stop you from leaving?"

"What will stop me now?"

"I will."

She shivered despite the warmth of her Thinsulate jacket. She'd like to retort, *him and what army,* but she suspected he wouldn't need an army. And if he did, he could summon one with no problem.

"Why? What do you want from me?"

Using only one arm, he held the weighty box with which she'd struggled while he brushed his black hair back with his other hand. "Right now all I want is to help you."

At the risk of sounding like her son, she wanted to ask why again. But although she didn't remember Evan Quade, she'd already learned something about him. He was a man of responsibility. He might not be in love with her anymore, but having her wear his ring once upon a time made him feel responsible for her.

She swallowed hard, realizing she'd almost accepted what he'd told her as fact. If he were her husband, that would make him Christopher's father. And what about Christopher? What did this man feel for his son?

A gasp slipped through her lips. She had never considered Christopher as anyone's but hers. Could she share him? Was that what Evan Quade wanted? Or would he want it all? His strong personality definitely demanded all or nothing.

"I can handle this." Maybe if she said the words enough times, she would begin to believe them. Right now she had serious doubts.

"How? By running?" he asked archly.

"Yes." She lifted her chin, feeling no shame in her cowardice. She'd lost the woman who'd bravely fought off her assailant. She'd lost that woman just as she'd lost this man. And she harbored no hope of recovering either.

He chuckled. "I don't believe in running. I never did. The best way to deal with things is to face them head-on. That's why I visited the prison this morning."

Fear whipped through her at the memory of her one visit there. Voice trembling, she asked, "You saw him?"

He nodded, his hard mouth pressed into a grim line.

"And?"

"You're in danger."

Although she had known it already, hearing him say it stole away that glimmer of hope she had held on to despite the odds. "Don't you see? That's why I have to leave. And you can't stop me!"

She jerked the box from his arm and stomped over to the van to slide it next to the others.

"I could if I wanted to. We both know that. I have certain legal rights I've been denied, Amanda."

She shivered more over the coldness of his words

than the chilled wind. She straightened up and blinked back tears before she turned to face him again.

His handsome face bore no expression, the dark eyes shadowed with secrets only he knew. "I have people working on finding his cell mate and confirming the threats. Give me some time, Amanda."

"And if I don't?"

He shook his head and she could read the frustration now.

"Damn, you're still so stubborn…"

Stubbornness was a sign of strength, so maybe she still had some left. But desperation brought forth the lie. "Christopher has an all-day field trip today. When he gets home, I'm leaving."

"You're only giving me until late afternoon?"

Before she could reply, a shout from the SUV drew Evan's attention.

"Evan! I got a lead! Come on!"

He turned back. "I'm going to check this out. If you need me…"

He dug into the pocket of his overcoat and withdrew a gold-embossed business card. "My cell phone number's on there. And I'm staying at the River City Plaza."

She widened her eyes over the expense of that, but then she shifted her gaze to the idling sports car. He had money, influence…all the vices her attacker had possessed, in her opinion.

With a trembling hand she took the card and shoved it into her pocket. Maybe he *could* help her, but she wasn't going to risk sticking around to find out. "Go ahead. Follow your lead."

He nodded and jaunted across the road to the sports car.

She waited until both vehicles had pulled away from the curb and disappeared around the corner before she slammed the cargo doors. Then she slid behind the wheel.

She'd packed all she had time and room to take with her. Now she had to pick up Christopher from school. She'd allowed him one last day, knowing he was safe while the convict still resided behind bars where he belonged.

Once she had Christopher they would head out of River City, the only home she remembered. And according to the man who claimed to be her husband, the only home she'd ever had.

Fingers numbed from the cold slid the key into the ignition and turned. A spinning noise and metallic clank drifted from under the hood, but no rumble of the motor springing to life.

Nothing.

Not again.

She shifted against the seat and a corner of the business card stabbed into her leg. No flimsy paper for him. Unbendable, just like the man.

Of course. He'd had his friend sabotage the van. Anger bubbled up and threatened to explode in a scream. She contained it but slammed the door after jumping down from the driver's seat.

Unlatching the hood was a familiar action, which she did by rote. But looking at the motor revealed no secrets. This time the cables were attached to the battery. What else could he have done to prevent it from starting?

Out of habit she reached for the diamond necklace, but it was gone. Pawned that morning. Now she had money—money she'd intended to use to start a new life for Christopher and herself—and she'd have to use it to repair or replace her vehicle. Doing either would take time, time she didn't have.

She blinked back tears of frustration and turned to Mrs. Olson's house across the street where a curtain swished at a window.

Stubborn, Evan had called her. He had no idea. And until now, neither had she. She wasn't going to lose another day of running. He could chase down leads. She would chase freedom from the animal that was getting out of prison and freedom from her "husband."

THE STOP WAS UNSCHEDULED. Not that she'd really scheduled anything.

She certainly hadn't anticipated the extra time and expense of begging Mrs. Olson to coerce her mechanic son to get the van in right away to his repair shop. But for an extra fifty, he'd quickly replaced the worn-out starter, something he'd warned her some time ago had to be done—something she wished she had gotten fixed before.

And something Evan Quade could not have tampered with.

So she had judged him a bit too harshly. She didn't intend to apologize.

What she had intended was to get the heck out of town once her van was running again.

So why had she gone to the D.A.'s office? Could it be she had some faith in Evan Quade, that she be-

lieved he could prevent the release of the prisoner
who had stolen her life?

Only the D.A. would know for sure.

Peter Sullivan closed the office door behind his
back after stepping into the hall with her. Amanda
peered around his shoulder through the glass door and
saw her son bent over, furiously scribbling on a legal
pad at the D.A.'s desk. When she'd picked him up
from school, he had refused to talk to her. He didn't
want to leave his home. Neither did she.

"Who *is* he?" Amanda asked, turning her attention
to the D.A.

"Evan Quade?" Sullivan jerked at the knot of his
paisley tie. "Who he says he is."

Her breath caught and burned in her throat. "My
husband?"

"Yes."

"So I am Amanda Quade?"

"Legally Caroline Quade, but you never used your
legal name. That's why we couldn't match you to the
missing person report he'd filed on you. The police
in Chicago hadn't filled out the report completely.
They hadn't included your nickname. And because of
the attack and your memory loss, we didn't release
any information about you. For your safety. You're
so vulnerable."

Because she'd lost her mind.

"We really didn't go looking for people to claim
you. We felt it would have been better if your memory had returned on its own. Safer."

Safety. An oxymoron. She'd never be safe once
authorities set a killer free.

"Maybe we should have divulged more information. Maybe we should have looked for a husband."

But she'd never suspected she'd been married. She'd even told him so—on several occasions. Even now she couldn't accept that she'd been that wrong. Couldn't accept that she belonged with Evan Quade.

Absently she lifted her hand to her neck but pulled it back when she remembered the necklace was gone. Just like the life she'd lived as Mrs. Quade. But that was the past and now she had to concentrate on the future. "He wants to help me. He's trying to find the guy who broke into my van."

Sullivan nodded. "He has more resources than the city does. He's hired all the experts and I'm sure he will find him. Now getting the man to testify…"

"So he hasn't found him yet?"

The D.A. shook his head.

She swallowed her disappointment that his lead hadn't panned out. "There isn't enough time. I have to leave."

"You're going with him?"

She shivered. "No. I can't trust him. I still don't remember him."

Sullivan's eyes widened. "What does it matter when he's offering you protection, Amanda? He can protect you."

"From Weering. But who will protect me from him?"

"He's an honorable man. I checked him out. His brother-in-law is the Winter Falls sheriff."

"Brother-in-law?" Why did that seem wrong to her? Could the past be as locked away in her mind as she believed?

''You think he's lying? I called and spoke directly with the sheriff, who swears Quade's who he says he is. Quade is something of a hero in that town, brought it financial prosperity. Not only would your husband protect you, but the local law enforcement would, too. You would be safe there.''

Physically. But once again, where her husband was concerned, her fear was of the emotional harm he could do her.

She glanced up to see the D.A. had turned toward his office again. A smile softened his lined face. ''And Christopher would be safe there.''

Hearing his words left her no choice. Reluctantly she shoved her fingers into her pocket and fingered the card—her means of contacting a husband she couldn't remember.

But she dialed other numbers while Mr. Sullivan and Christopher ate cookies in the hall. She double-checked the D.A.'s assessment, calling the sheriff he'd talked to as well as Evan's office number. His secretary verified his identity.

Maybe she could trust him to protect her and her son from physical harm at a madman's hands. But the only person who could protect her from emotional harm from her husband was herself, and she doubted she was strong enough. She doubted she had ever been strong enough to handle him, his powerful personality or the powerful feelings he inspired.

He'd said she ran away from him once. She must have had a reason to run. When the threat to her and her son's life was gone, would she be able to leave him again?

Now that he knew about Christopher, would he let

her walk out of his life as she once had? Or would he fight her for his son?

Tension throbbed at the base of her skull as she accepted that only one person could answer her questions: her husband.

Chapter Four

Evan stared out over the river as he idly ran a diamond necklace through his fingers. "This makes sense."

He gestured toward the murky water many floors below the hotel-suite window. The diamonds glittered in the late-afternoon sun and bounced back shards of light at Royce's reflection in the glass.

"Hmm?" Royce didn't glance up from the report cradled in his hand, but he leaned back in the chair at the small cherry-wood table.

"River City. City named for the river. I've lived in Winter Falls a couple of years now and I don't know why it's named that. Do you?"

"Must be a reason… I'll ask Sarah tonight. And instead of wasting time reading these reports and transcripts, you should tell me what's in here. We wasted enough time today chasing down that dead end. Martin 'Snake' Timmer hasn't showed up at the warehouse for work in over a week."

Evan dragged in a deep breath, refusing to let the frustration overtake him.

"Tracking his social-security number didn't show

where he's applied for another job, either,'' Royce continued, anger sharpening his tone.

Someone had paid off the "witness." Evan didn't need confirmation of what he knew in his gut.

Royce sighed. "Damn it! So just tell me what's in these reports. Finding something in here to link that bastard to other crimes might be the only way to keep him behind bars. You glanced at these, they're permanently in your mind now."

And that was the curse of Evan's photographic memory. Those words from the trial had already become images in his head, images he wouldn't forget as Amanda had. *As she'd forgotten him,* he thought to himself.

He concentrated on his breathing as he sought calmness, control. He should have broken his neck for what that bastard had done to her.

"He kept her in that trunk for hours, at least. Maybe a day or more…"

Royce tossed one file down and grabbed up another. "One of the shrinks says that she's terrified of the dark. Can't say I blame her."

"She was so dehydrated, she should have been weak. Pliable. That's what he was counting on…" Evan's voice trailed off. But that wasn't what the animal had gotten. She'd fought. For their child. When she'd awoken in the hospital days later, the one thing she hadn't forgotten was her pregnancy.

Had she known when she'd left him? Had she known then that she'd carried his child? And if so, why had she left?

Because she hadn't loved him, he realized. Hadn't loved him enough to even remember him now…

Evan shook off the self-pity and said, "Let's forget about what's done already, Royce, and concentrate on now." The diamond necklace gnawed at his fingers as he wrapped it around his knuckles. "You trust this security firm?"

Royce nodded, but his eyes narrowed and scrutinized.

Evan turned away from his too perceptive friend and focused on the river again. "They've been watching her?"

"Yeah, that's how they knew she'd pawned the necklace this morning. And tomorrow when he's released, they'll be watching him. You have it all under control, Evan."

Evan laughed, but no humor lifted the heaviness from his chest. "Control? I haven't had that since I knocked on her door yesterday."

"You're doing everything you can—"

"Everything she'll let me." Despite her loss of memory, she was the same stubborn woman he'd been married to, was still married to.

Until death did them part, he'd vowed at their wedding. But since then he'd learned the truth about himself, about *what* he'd come from. After what she'd been through, how would the truth affect her?

Royce expelled a ragged sigh. "If only we'd gotten Timmer…"

"Snake slithered away from us." Evan resisted the urge to smash his fist against the glass in an expression of the anger and frustration churning inside him.

"But at least we know who gave Amanda the warning. We need to track down where he moved to next. We can still find him in time. We have people watching his daughter's house to see if he shows up there.''

Evan groaned over Royce's positive new attitude. Marital bliss had stolen some of the tough cynicism that Evan had first admired about the ex-FBI agent.

''You think his message was a warning?''

''Yeah, Sullivan wasn't going to tell her the creep was getting out. He figured she'd freak and run off.''

''Exactly.''

''Ah…'' The chair creaked as Royce jumped up and joined Evan at the window. ''So you think Weering set this up? Probably paid his old buddy to warn Amanda, so she'd run.''

Evan nodded. ''Control. He wants it over her. Fear. He thrives on that. He wants her scared and he wants to orchestrate her every move. And the bastard's winning right now.''

Royce settled a hand on Evan's shoulder, squeezing. ''But he didn't count on you.''

He closed his eyes, and an image of the half-blinded convict sneered in his mind. ''I'm not so sure.''

''You mean because he knows things…''

''Things only people close to me know, Royce.'' Things Evan wished he didn't know himself. If only…

No, ''if only'' would have kept him from the family he loved. His sister, his sweet baby niece and the friends he had made when his adoptive parents had disowned him after Amanda's disappearance, which they had considered too suspicious. They had even shared their concerns with the local police department. If the people who had raised him had thought he could harm her...

Royce rationalized, "We aren't the only ones that know about your biological father. There's a trail. There's always a trail."

He hoped Royce was right. "We have to find Weering's."

"We're checking the files. If we can link him to other crimes... Damn, why wouldn't they wait on releasing him?"

Evan curled his hands into fists. He had tried bribes, threats, but nothing had swayed the bureaucrats. "They're trying to justify what they've done. They refuse to believe they're releasing someone who hasn't been fully rehabilitated."

"And when he hurts someone? How are they gonna save face then?"

Evan's knuckles turned white. "He *won't* hurt Amanda...or the boy."

The boy. His stomach pitched. His son. He had a son. Their one brief meeting played again and again in his head. The child with the dark eyes full of lively intelligence peering up at him...

His son.

But would the kid look up to him if he knew what only Evan's friends and a soon-to-be released prisoner knew? If not for an act of violence Evan wouldn't even exist. How would Amanda, a victim of violence, ever accept that her husband was a product of that? Accept he had a rapist's blood running through his veins?

"You're doing everything you can," Royce said.

But Royce's reassurance didn't calm Evan's fears.

"I can do more. I have to get through to her this time."

He turned from the window, grabbing up his camel overcoat from the back of a chair before heading out. Full of fierce determination, he yanked open the door and nearly bowled over the small fragile woman and the little boy standing in the hall.

"Amanda?" Evan asked, shocked by her appearance at his hotel room.

"Did you find him yet?" she asked, her eyes full of tentative hope.

He didn't need to ask of whom she spoke. Although he hated to dash that hope, nevertheless he shook his head. "No. It was a dead end. Bad lead."

Her teeth nipped at her full bottom lip as she nodded, and the hope in her eyes vanished. He expected her to turn and run, instead she stammered, "That's what Mr. Sullivan said, but... Uh...Ev...Mr. Quade..."

Regret was added to the burden lying heavy over his heart. Amanda didn't even know what to call him, this woman who had vowed to love him forever.

He regretted her lost memory. Only he would ever know of the passion they'd once shared. The way she'd whispered his name and reached for him in the dark. The way her silky naked skin, slick with sweat from their passion, had slid over his as she'd moved against him in the night.

He swallowed hard. "It's ridiculous for you to call me by my last name when it's one we share."

"Our last name is Smith." Christopher spoke up, his voice soft and his dark eyes wide with curiosity.

Hell, what was in a name anyways? Evan thought.

He would never use the surname that was biologically his. He found himself hunkering down before Christopher, but even on his haunches he was too big to meet the child eye to eye. "You're smart."

Christopher nodded, his curls tousling around his face. "Yup."

Evan couldn't laugh at the boy's arrogance, not when it was something undoubtedly inherited from him. This was his child. His flesh and blood. "What else do you know?"

The boy lifted his thin shoulders. "Lots of stuff. My phone number and address…"

His little rounded chin wobbled, and his bottom lip, full like Amanda's, trembled. "But it's not our house anymore."

Evan lifted his gaze to Amanda's face. Her green eyes shimmered with unshed tears. His stomach clenched, and he glanced away at the watch on his wrist. "His all-day field trip end early?"

From the bodyguard he had hired to follow her, he knew she had intended to leave the house right after he and Royce had. He also knew the van had broken down and required repairs. How much did she have left of the pawn money from the necklace?

She leaned closer, close enough that her scent washed over him. Peaches and cream wafted from her short tresses. He liked it better than the expensive musk she used to wear. "I lied," she whispered.

He nodded and straightened up, putting some distance between them with a step back. Dropping his coat onto the sofa, he turned to Royce. "I don't think you've been introduced. Amanda, this is Royce Graham, 'The Tracker.'"

She shivered, probably imagining having a child lost and needing this man to find him. "The FBI agent?"

Royce sighed. "Used to be. Now I work for my-self…and my friends." He stepped closer to where Evan's wife and child hovered in the doorway. "Hey, little man, you should see this game I have. I bor-rowed it from my son. It's pretty awesome. I have it in my room."

Evan appreciated his friend's interference. Al-though he had some experience with children, Evan could hardly talk to this one, not with all the emotions battering him. "Christopher, I bet you'd like to see that game. And, Amanda, if Royce takes him in his room, then you and I would have some time to talk."

With wide eyes her expressive face telegraphed her fear of being alone with Evan and her reluctance to be parted from her child. Her fingers tousled his hair in an unconsciously loving gesture.

"Didn't you come here to talk to me? Do you want him to hear?" Evan prodded gently.

"What kind of game?" Christopher asked.

Royce chuckled. "Something with lots of bright colors."

"I don't want him to see anything violent," Amanda said, her voice quavering.

Evan hoped he would never have to. "He shouldn't hear about any violence either, Amanda."

She nodded. "You can go with Mr. Graham, Chris-topher. Mind your manners, though."

"It's golf—the only way I have time to play it," Royce clarified, taking the boy's chubby fingers in his and leading him to a door off the living room of the suite.

At the threshold the little boy glanced back at Evan, a question in his dark eyes. *He knows. He knows I'm his father.* Staggered by the thought Evan settled heavily onto the sofa as Royce and Christopher exited to the next room.

"What have you told him?" he asked after the door had closed safely behind the pair.

"About leaving town?"

"About me." Evan was unsure if he had ever intended to tell the boy that he was his son. What did he have to offer him? What kind of father could he ever be? After steadying it with an effort, he plowed a hand through his hair. "But since you brought it up, what *did* you tell him about leaving town, leaving his school, his house, his friends?"

She trembled as she crossed the room to the windows overlooking the river. "I said that we had to go. That it was time."

"He's a smart kid. I doubt he accepted that for an answer."

"What else could I tell him? He's five years old. I couldn't tell him the truth." She choked and swallowed hard, lowering her voice. "I couldn't tell him we were leaving for his protection. Like I told you last night, he threw a tantrum, so no, he didn't accept it. He still doesn't. He wants to stay."

"But you don't."

"I can't!" After the outburst she pressed a fist against her lips.

Evan stood up and strode over to the windows, too. Despite the inclination to offer comfort, to offer a shoulder on which she could release the tears that were shimmering in her enormous green eyes, he kept a few feet of distance between them. Breathing room. "So why are you here?"

He knew she hadn't remembered anything about their past, about him. She still stared at him with a stranger's wariness, or worse, a victim's.

After spending some of the little money she had on the van repairs, was she desperate enough to ask him for more? "What do you need, Amanda?"

She blinked hard and the tears stayed at bay. "Answers."

"You want to know about the past now?" Last night and the day before, she'd said she had no time or interest in it.

She shook her head and stepped closer to him, delineating the careful distance he'd kept between them. "Not all of it. I want to know about you."

Why she'd left him? She would probably ask for the one answer he didn't have—for the one he'd searched six years for—and due to her memory loss, would probably never know.

He dragged in a deep breath. "Ask away."

Her gaze dropped to his chest to where the ring burned beneath his shirt, reminding him, always reminding him how damn bad love hurt. "I know that…we were…married," she said after a moment.

He ignored the painful twitch of the muscle in his jaw and continued to clench it to bone-shattering intensity. "And?"

"I know who you are. That you're an influential man with important friends…like Mr. Graham…and others… I've talked to the Winter Falls sheriff."

The devil prodded him to say, "He's my sister's husband. He could be lying for me."

"About what?"

He shrugged. "I don't know. About my being a good man."

"He never called you that." Beneath her shaggy bangs, her forehead puckered. "In fact, nobody I talked to called you that."

He swallowed a groan. "Is that what you want to know?"

She shook her head again. "No, they called you honorable. That's close enough. And that's really what I want."

"My honor?"

"Yes." She licked her lips, her tongue swiping over her full bottom lip and nearly undoing Evan's fragile control. "I want your word that if Christopher and I go with you to Winter Falls that you will protect us."

Just like the old Amanda, she had managed to stagger him. "What? You're going to trust me?"

Touched by her faith, he slid his fingers along her taut cheekbone and into the hair feathering her ear. She flinched under his touch, so he dropped his hand. "No, you don't trust me."

"I want to." The words were uttered as an anguished moan, and again the tears shimmered. "I really want to, but I can't remember anything. I can't remember if I should trust you. I can't remember you…"

Feelings pummeled Evan's restraint. He'd once loved her so much, once shared everything with this woman, all his hopes, fears and passion. And she remembered nothing.

Nothing of him.

But since finding her again, he hadn't acted like the lovesick fool he'd once been for her. He'd leashed his emotions because he'd known he'd found her with the sole intention of letting her go. But he couldn't let her go now, not yet, not when a madman intended to hurt her.

Overcome by an unexpected surge of protectiveness, he then found himself taking her soft mouth in a hard kiss as his restraint snapped. His lips plundered, his tongue delving into the sweet recesses of her mouth when she gasped. One of his hands held the nape of her neck while the other ran over her slender back, grasping at the suedelike material of her jacket.

When her hands clutched at his hair, he fought for his senses, knowing she probably wanted to pull him off. Instead, her fingers tightened, and her lips returned his kiss, her tongue sliding along his.

Deep breathing was impossible with the way his heart pounded. Despite the years, she tasted the same, just as sweet with passion. Exactly as he remembered but more…

He gentled the kiss, his mouth caressing hers as his fingers ran through her short silky tresses. He'd just touched the hard ridge of a scar beneath her hair when she swayed in his arms. Had she fainted again?

"Evan!"

The voice that called his name wasn't hers. She didn't call him Evan. She called him Mr. Quade. His wife treated him like a stranger.

She pulled out of his arms as Royce poked his head out of the door to his room. "Sorry, man, but you didn't hear the phone…"

Evan fought to clear the passion from his brain as Amanda turned to the window, her back to him and her arms wrapped protectively around her midriff. What had he done? She'd just agreed to try to trust him and he'd destroyed that, destroyed whatever chance he'd had of convincing her to come willingly to Winter Falls.

When the trial transcripts and medical records flashed behind the eyes he squeezed closed, he knew he would bring her home with him—no matter what resistance she put up.

"Evan," Royce said again.

He shook his head, clearing it of the jumbled words and emotions. "Yeah, phone. Who is it?"

"Cullen Murphy." A member of the River City security firm they'd hired. "He found Snake."

"Is he with Cullen?"

"No, Cullen just called with the address to see what we wanted to do."

"We want to talk to Snake." God, he hoped it wasn't another dead end. "Let's go."

He didn't want to leave Amanda alone, but then another Murphy watched her. She wouldn't get far without Evan's knowledge, or without Evan himself. He wasn't taking any chances on losing Amanda again.

"I'm going with you," she said, her voice steely with determination.

AMANDA DIDN'T KNOW what surprised her more. That she'd convinced Evan Quade to let her come along to confront Snake, or that she'd agreed to leave her son in a stranger's care. But then again, The Tracker was no stranger to any parent. He was the first one you would call if you lost your child. Wouldn't he be the best choice to keep Christopher safe? Probably a better choice than she was.

And Evan trusted him. Amanda doubted many people earned his trust. From looking into the intensity of his dark eyes, she wondered if she ever would. If she'd had it once, it seemed she'd destroyed whatever chance she'd had of keeping it. Of keeping *him.*

What was she thinking? She wanted nothing from him but his protection.

His taste lingered yet on her lips. Rich and dark like her favorite chocolate. But there'd been nothing sweet about the way he'd grabbed her, taking…what had once been his. What still was unless he'd divorced her on grounds of desertion.

Had she deserted him? If so, why? Or had she known then, with her memory intact, that they had nothing in common? He was so dark and intense, and she… She had no idea what she'd once been, but now she was afraid of the dark.

Evan hadn't spoken to her since he'd given his consent for her to come along. His hands gripped the steering wheel of his powerful sports car, the engine rumbling with such quiet intensity that she felt the vibrations. Or was that still the passion that had hummed through her veins when he'd so briefly held her in his arms?

Amanda had to shake off the memory of that kiss, had to banish it to the dark abyss where the rest of her memories of this man resided. But had something surfaced with his kiss? Some familiarity? She refused to dwell on it. Trying to remember never accomplished anything but a debilitating headache.

Although the calendar declared it spring, the weather didn't know it. Winter gloom lingered, prematurely darkening the afternoon. Night still fell too soon and in a couple of short hours, total darkness would reign.

She shuddered.

"Change your mind?" he asked, missing nothing although he hadn't taken his gaze from the road.

"No. I really believe he won't talk to you." She could hardly bring herself to talk to Evan, and a marriage license called this dark intimidating man her husband. "I can remind him of what he said, that he has a daughter my age, that he would protect her. There's a better chance that I can get him to talk to the police."

She prayed she could. Christopher's future—and hers—depended on it for more than safety.

For sanity.

Amanda feared going to Winter Falls with this man. Although it might be the only way to ensure her physical survival, she doubted she would survive emotionally, since just a kiss had made her so weak-kneed, she'd almost fainted in his arms. Again.

"I wasn't talking about seeing Snake," Evan said, interrupting her thoughts. With the care of an expert, he rounded a corner at a speed she would have considered too great. The van would have rolled. But then this expensive machine was not her dilapidated old van. And she didn't have an ounce of the confidence this man displayed.

Was he really that confident?

"You were talking about Christopher and I going with you to Winter Falls?"

She studied his chiseled profile and noted the flare of his nostrils as he inhaled deeply, like the deep-breathing maneuver taught to her by a psychiatrist.

"Did you change your mind?" he asked.

She pretended to consider his question although she already knew she had.

"I shouldn't have kissed you," he said.

She waited for an apology, not sure what she'd do with it. Had she regretted the kiss? It had been so long since she'd been touched. And since her attack— in all the time she could remember—she'd never been kissed at all, let alone with such passion.

Consumed. He had consumed her but she'd responded. She'd clutched him to her and returned the passion. Her body hummed with it yet. Although her mind had forgotten him, her body had not. "If you thought it'd make me remember you…"

"I failed." His voice deepened to a husky murmur with the admission.

For a moment, she wondered if he was talking about only the kiss?

"That kiss doesn't matter anymore." She winced over the lie. "Once this man talks to the police, tells them about the threat, you said you'd be able to keep that animal behind bars."

He nodded. "And Royce is working with the Feds on the other cases where Weering was a suspect. If they can find anything to link him to those crimes…"

She shivered, thinking again of how lucky she'd been to live through her attack. What was a memory in comparison to a life or the life of her then unborn child? But what those other women must have suffered… "How can they even consider letting him out?"

"Money and power."

Resentment coursed through her. As his wife, she had probably had those things, too. But as a victim, she'd become poor and powerless. "You'd know."

With a glance across her to the mirror, he effortlessly parallel parked at the curb of a run-down apartment complex. "Yeah, I would."

Again the admission was uttered in a way that made her think he was saying more. Had she lost her perception with her memory? And her objectivity?

When he turned toward the car door, she clutched at the sleeve of his overcoat until he swung back. "I'm sorry. That wasn't fair. You're not like him. It was cruel of me—"

"Don't apologize. There're things you don't know about me." His dark eyes churned with emotion and a muscle jumped in his clenched jaw.

"Things I've forgotten."

"Things you never knew, Amanda. Things *I* never knew."

She shivered despite the warmth in the close confines of the small car. With a trembling hand she fumbled with the catch for the door. "We…"

Needed to talk. To each other maybe more than this tattooed ex-convict. But they'd have time later. Wouldn't they?

"We need to go inside. Let's hope he didn't see

us drive up. Looks like the entrance is around the corner." He leaned over and opened her car door before she could figure out the handle. His gaze intent on her face, he said, "Maybe you should stay here. Let me talk to him first."

"I told you—"

"He could be dangerous, Amanda."

"Then he would have hurt me in the van. He didn't. He warned me."

"But that could have been part of the plan."

"Plan?" Foreboding crawled along her skin, raising goose bumps, so she shifted closer to Evan's heat.

"Weering's plan to make you run, to take you away from the people who could protect you."

"You think he's planned this?" She clutched at his sleeve again, needing the reassurance of his strong presence.

"He's had nearly six years with little else to think about. Yeah, I think he has a plan."

Despite the fear, the intensity of which would have normally paralyzed her, desperation inspired her to action. Any action. Anything that would keep that animal away from her. "Let's go," she said, climbing from the sports car and walking toward the entrance.

She kept close to the building where white paint peeled off the brick and flaked onto the cracked sidewalk. The rubber soles of her running shoes were silent on the cement, as were Evan's leather loafers. Although music and voices drifted through the thin-paned windows and onto the street and, in the distance, police sirens and car horns blared, she felt isolated.

But for Evan.

When they rounded the corner, he stepped in front of her, opening the door to the building and staring intently at her as she passed through it. His rich scent washed over her, the woods and leather fragrance camouflaging some of the garbage and urine odor of the foyer.

"You still want to talk to him first?" she asked, a bit fearful of this place unlike anywhere she'd ever been. She hadn't known there were areas this deplorable in River City.

He nodded as he peered up the graffiti-covered stairwell to the next floor. "This isn't a safe place, Amanda."

"Then I wouldn't be safe waiting in the car, either. And I know I can get through to him." She wouldn't feel safe in the car by herself, as dusk fell outside. Surprisingly, only at Evan's side did the fear ease somewhat. But to totally ease her fear, she'd need to convince Martin "Snake" Timmer to help her.

Despite the narrowness they climbed the steps side by side, nearly in sync despite the disparity in the lengths of their legs. Amanda smiled over her ability to keep up with him until she realized he had slowed up for her, protecting her, his body tense and shielding.

He pressed close to her as they walked down the littered corridor toward Snake's room on the fourth floor. Nobody glanced out into the hall, not like her neighbors who hovered behind sheer curtains watching out for her. This was the kind of place where nobody wanted to see anything. And from the volume of TVs and stereos inside their apartments, they didn't want to hear anything, either.

She shuddered as Evan stopped at the last door along the corridor. ''According to Murphy, this is it.'' He lifted his hand to knock, but the door creaked open before he had applied any pressure.

First she saw the snake. The tattoo could have come to life and slithered across the floor for all the detail in the brilliant colors of the permanent ink. Only one color was more brilliant than the browns and blacks and the yellow of the beady eyes.

Red.

Not the red of the tongue flickering between the fangs.

The red of the blood that poured from Snake's head wounds and gushed onto the worn vinyl floor.

She screamed, a mere squeak of horror, not enough to drown out the clang of steps on the fire escape outside Snake's open window.

Evan didn't stand frozen in terror as she did. He checked for a pulse beneath the mutilated face. At the noise he turned to the open window. And before she could clutch his sleeve again to hold him back, Evan slipped over the sill and into the gloom of dusk.

In pursuit of a killer.

For there was no doubt in her mind that Snake was dead despite the blood still flowing from the empty sockets where his eyes had been only a short while ago.

He would bear no witness to the threat against her. He would bear no witness ever again.

Chapter Five

"Evan!"

Despite the terror in her voice, Evan didn't turn back. He knew Snake couldn't hurt her, couldn't hurt anyone.

But below Evan, a dark-clothed figure fled down the fire escape. A ski mask covered the person's head, and in a gloved hand, a bloodied knife glinted in the fading light.

Evan's footsteps pounded on the metal treads as he pursued the killer, closing in on him on the last landing. Without turning around, the man reached back, slashing the knife through the air. Blood smeared Evan's overcoat.

Falling back on years of training, he kicked out and sent the knife arcing into the air. The murder weapon landed with a clatter onto the landing above. To retrieve it the killer would have to go through him.

Evan widened his stance, but the figure didn't turn back. Instead he leaped off the landing and into the alley. With an expulsion of air and an oath, he rolled across the asphalt, regaining his feet to run again.

Evan jumped, too, effortlessly finding his feet beneath him. But during the leap he had taken his gaze from the killer. No flash of dark clothes could be distinguished from the shadows as late afternoon slipped into evening.

A truck engine ground to life, the rumble of it nearly drowning out the sounds of Amanda's footsteps on the fire escape. He glanced up at her, opening his mouth to tell her to call 911 when she screamed again.

''Evan!''

The truck, a four-wheel-drive pickup complete with lift kit to increase its height, jumped the curb and headed toward him. The retractable ladder to the escape dangled nine feet above the ground, but Evan leaped for it, his fingers closing around a steel rung just as the truck swerved to miss the building. His foot brushed against the front fender as he clamored up to safety.

The danger passed as the truck sped off, engine roaring down the street as the killer escaped. ''Damn it!''

''Are you okay?'' Amanda's voice shook and tears streaked down her face. ''I called the police. I called.''

Evan joined her on the landing. The metal vibrated beneath him as he shook with the rush of adrenaline. He reached for Amanda to assure himself of her safety.

She reached out, too, for his coat, blood smearing her fingers when she ran them over it. Horror reverberated in her voice. ''You're bleeding!''

''It's not my blood. I'm not hurt,'' he assured her, pulling her into an embrace.

"But you rushed out after him... He could have...done to you what he did to..." She trembled in his arms, undoubtedly in shock from what she'd seen.

"I'm fine. Nothing happened to me. Are you all right?" God, he wished he had not let her come along with him, wished she hadn't had to see what had been done to Snake.

She shook her head, biting at her lip even as she pulled away. "No, I'm scared. That was him, Evan. He's out."

"No. Not until tomorrow..."

But then who had committed this murder?

Money and power. Money and power could buy anything—even a killer for a killer.

Or one less day?

He fumbled inside his coat pocket, pulling out his cell phone and a business card. Since it was past five, he dialed the D.A.'s cell number. "This is Quade."

The older man's sigh carried gustily through the phone. "I've been trying to reach you. I can't find Amanda. I was hoping she was with you."

"You're hoping that she's safe." Evan felt the way she trembled uncontrollably beside him. "He's out, isn't he?"

"Yes, damn it!"

"How?"

"I don't know. He probably paid for a new wing for the prison."

"And he needs to be put back in it. He got somebody already."

"Who? Amanda's okay, isn't she?"

"She is." For now. He couldn't say it, couldn't

doubt her safety. "But Martin 'Snake' Timmer isn't. He's been murdered, and I know the prime suspect."

"You saw him?"

The coward hadn't shown his face, and a dark stocking cap had covered his signature pale hair. "Come on, we all know who did this."

"We need proof, damn it. All I can do now is have him brought in for questioning."

"Then do it!" He slammed the phone shut and thrust it back into his pocket, nearly tearing the fabric with the force of his action. But it wasn't enough. He needed to do *more*. A few deep breaths brought him some calm but not enough.

Next to him, Amanda stilled and lifted her chin. "He *is* out?"

Evan wanted to lie, wanted to do anything that would stop the rise of hysteria into her expressive eyes. But she needed to know. "Yes."

Her teeth sank into her lip, and she nodded. "I knew it. I knew…" She glanced up the fire escape to the open window and shuddered. "I knew it was him."

On some level so had Evan.

The wail of sirens as the police cars pulled to the curb nearly drowned out her comment. "Money and power…"

She obviously knew how Weering had gotten out another day early.

He had no problem hearing her next words as she nearly screamed. "Christopher. I have to make sure Christopher's okay."

"He's fine. Royce has him."

She jerked at his arm, her fingers tangling in the

fabric of his coat. "No, you don't understand. He killed this man to get to me, to hurt me…. The eyes…what he did to his eyes…that was a message to me!"

A message Evan had heard loud and clear. "Yes, it was."

An eye for an eye…

"He's going to go after Christopher next! I know it!" Hysteria pitched her voice high and she shook with fear. "We have to leave. We have to go to him! We have to protect our son, Evan!"

Our son. His heart clenched with some of her fear. But Christopher was safe and would remain so—he would see to it. *Nothing* could happen to that little boy…for Amanda's sake and *his.*

Evan suppressed a shudder and pulled Amanda's trembling body into his arms as the police approached them on the sidewalk. Over her hitching sobs, he told them what they had witnessed. But he couldn't bring Amanda back into that building, into the gruesome scene of carnage. "The murder weapon is on the fire escape. I doubt you'll find any prints. He was wearing gloves." Evan finished as she sobbed into his chest.

"Please…we have to leave…" she begged.

With a killer on the loose, they had no choice.

FOR ONCE AMANDA WAS grateful for money and power…when it belonged to Evan Quade. Whatever he told the police enabled them to leave the crime scene after answering only a couple of questions.

William Weering III had killed that man, her one hope to keep the animal behind bars. She knew that. The police knew that. But just as it was six years ago, in order to lock him away for the right amount of time—forever—they needed evidence.

He was too smart to leave any. And too evil to give up and move on until he had completely destroyed her with his own hands. The fastest way to achieve that goal—hurt her son.

Once the light flashed green on the lock of the hotel suite, her hands closed over Evan's and pushed open the door. "Christopher! Christopher! Mommy's back!"

Why had she left him with a stranger? No matter how famous the man was for his care of children, Christopher wasn't his. And Amanda would never have forgiven herself for not being there if anything had happened to her little boy.

"Christopher!"

She skidded to a halt in the doorway to the ex-FBI agent's room. The screen of the TV in the armoire was filled with an image that had her cringing with fear.

Weering smiled at a reporter and winked his blind eye. "I thank Senator Van Dover for bringing a halt to the injustice against me in granting my early parole."

"Are you saying you were wrongly imprisoned, Mr. Weering?" the reporter asked.

He sighed with a martyr's long-suffering weariness. "The police overreacted and misinterpreted the facts. I picked up a transient, a hitchhiker, who tried to steal my car by force. As you can see by my face, I was the wounded party, but my attacker has gone free all these years while I served out a jail sentence for acting in self-defense. Do you call that justice?"

Amanda shivered over the argument she'd heard in the courtroom all those years ago. Despite having no memory, she'd never believed his story. She'd known she was not a transient. And Evan Quade had proven her right when he'd claimed her as his wife.

William Weering III flashed his smile again, the one that oozed evil instead of charm and answered his own question. "No, ma'am."

"Do you intend to seek justice now, Mr. Weering?"

He focused on the camera lens, and Amanda swore he stared directly at her. Then he winked again.

She pressed a fist against her lips to hold in a scream. "Evan!"

"I'm here. Amanda, I'm here."

When he enfolded her in his arms this time, she didn't cling and weep as she had at the murder scene. She had to hold it together. For Christopher. "Where are they, Evan? Did he get him already?"

A big hand brushed over her hair and kneaded the tense muscles in her nape. "No, they're safe. They're gone."

She pulled back, and the hand he had curved around her waist rustled with a piece of notebook paper. "Where? Where are they?"

"Royce left a note. When he saw the news, he took Christopher and headed directly to Winter Falls. He tried my cell to warn us, but in the excitement, I didn't check the message."

She turned back to the TV, but a weather map filled the screen now. "That was recorded. It had to be. That was him back at…"

He had been so close to her…with no shatterproof glass between them.

"I know. I know."

"He'll go after Christopher next," she said. Her arms ached to hold her little boy until he squirmed free, embarrassed over her mushiness.

"He may not. But if he does, Christopher will be protected."

"He'd hurt him to hurt me."

"He'll hurt *you.* I talked to him yesterday. He never mentioned the boy. Only you. He's obsessed with *you.*" Something flickered in Evan's dark eyes. She doubted it was fear, not after the way he'd followed a killer through an open window. But she knew there was more to his conversation with Weering.

"And what else?" she asked.

"Me."

"He knows you?"

Evan shook his head. "No, not personally. But he will. Before this is all over, Amanda, he'll know me well."

She stepped away from him, reminded of how little she knew of a man who had kissed her only hours before, a man whose last name she shared. "I don't know what to believe. I just know I have to be with my son. He'll be scared."

She glanced out the window but night had fallen, cloaking the glass in black. No stars twinkled. No moon shone. Gasping for shallow breaths, she focused on her son, off with a stranger for the first time without her. Despite what this man said, Christopher could be in danger. He needed his mother and she needed him.

"I want to leave now."

"They're probably almost there. And with Weering fixated on you, Christopher's probably safer being away from you."

She gasped, the idea of her presence endangering her son horrifying. "No."

"It'll take us four hours. And it's dark, Amanda."

She shivered over her fear spoken aloud and the fact that this man knew one of her greatest vulnerabilities. "I don't care," she lied. "I need to be with my son, need to see that he's safe."

"He is. Not only does Royce have him, but he also made sure one of the security guards we hired followed him in your vehicle. That way you'll have your things in Winter Falls."

Material things didn't matter. The attack had left her with nothing. No memory. No possessions but for the jewelry she'd pawned. And she'd didn't miss it. All she missed was Christopher.

His voice low and soothing as if he spoke to a frightened child, he continued assuring her, "I understand your fears—trust me, I do. But we've had an emotionally trying day, and you need to rest. To regroup so we can deal with Weering. We can stay here tonight and leave first thing in the morning."

"No!" She backed away from him, through the living room and toward the outside door. "If you won't drive me, I'll find him myself!"

"Amanda, that's what Weering wants you to do…run off by yourself, make yourself an easy target. He's waiting for you to do that."

The muscles he had briefly loosened in her neck tensed up, and pain gnawed at her temples. "Then maybe he knows me better than you do. He knows I won't be separated from my son. But you don't seem to know that. I may have lost my memory of you, but I doubt you really knew me at all."

His jaw cracked he clenched it so hard. "I didn't."

"So that's why I left you then?"

He lifted one broad shoulder and shrugged it. "I don't know why. I never knew why. All these years the only reason I could come up with was the fact that I wanted a child, and you didn't."

HE LIED. SHE COULDN'T consider the other alternative. That she might not have wanted Christopher, that she hadn't wanted to give her husband a child.

No.

She'd fought for her unborn child. She'd blinded a man to save herself and her baby.

He lied. And maybe that was why he'd relented and agreed to bring her to Winter Falls tonight. Either that or her near hysteria at being separated from her son had softened him.

She glanced over, studying his granite profile illuminated by the dashboard lights. Why would he lie? Was he hiding the real reason from her? Had he hurt her? She doubted he would have physically harmed her. She didn't feel that kind of fear, the kind of fear that paralyzed her with just the mention of Weering's name.

If he had hurt her, it must have been emotionally.

Had he cheated? Was he hiding his infidelity with this despicable lie?

His deep voice rumbled in harmony with the purring engine of the sports car. "You don't believe me."

"I love my son." Her hands knotted together in her lap, knuckles turned white with the anxiety coursing through her—fear for Christopher's safety and fear of the dark that engulfed the little car, isolating them in a world of supple leather and pale amber lights.

His dark gaze flickered over her, missing nothing, she suspected. "I don't doubt that."

Now. Although he'd left it off, she heard the word. What kind of woman had she once been? Had she forgotten herself for another reason than the trauma she had suffered at William Weering's cruel hands?

"What was…?" She couldn't ask about herself. She wasn't this woman from his past. She wasn't the wife he remembered. She knew that. And to ask about her was like asking about another woman, a stranger.

"What were you like?" His nostrils flared as he dragged in a deep breath. Almost imperceptible, but she caught the gesture, the method of controlling his emotions. She practiced that, too. Had she learned it from the shrinks, or had she already known it from him?

Did talking about the past upset him? Or just talking about her?

He sighed and his hands shifted on the steering wheel. "I thought you didn't want to know anything about the past."

"I didn't have time then. I do now." And she needed to concentrate on anything other than the darkness. His voice, deep and rumbly, provided a distraction.

"So what do you want to know?"

"What did I do? Did I have a career?"

He chuckled. "Career? I'd call it more a way of life. Your father is a fashion designer. You were his apprentice. Your mother is a model. You traveled your entire life, and I doubt you ever would have stopped…"

Bitterness had deepened his voice even more, and once again she heard the words he left unsaid. Out of pity for her situation or his own pride? She didn't know which she'd prefer, his pity or his pride.

"If not for the attack," she finished. "Now, I hate to travel. I can't see this life you're saying I lived. But I do sew. I must have learned it back then."

"Taking care of your father." He made no effort to hide the bitterness now. "Taking care of his business."

"You didn't like my parents?"

He sighed. "I didn't understand them."

"Or me?"

A dimple pierced his cheek when he grinned. "Least of all, you."

"Then why did you marry me?" For love? Somehow she doubted that.

The silence stretched between them, his gaze leaving the road only to scan the gauges. "We need gas. There's a station ahead."

She closed her eyes, preferring the darkness inside her to out. "You're not going to answer me."

Gravel crunched beneath the tires as he down-shifted and pulled off the road. "You don't believe me anyways."

She mulled that over as he stopped the car and stepped outside. Why couldn't she trust him? Because she never had? Because of something he'd done? Or because of what had been done to her at the hands of an animal?

She dragged in a calming breath and inhaled the scent of Evan, the rich woodsy leathery fragrance that instinctively she knew cost a fortune. As did his car and his clothes...

He opened the door again. "I'm going to get a coffee. Do you want anything?"

She nodded. "Coffee would be great. Cream—"

"And sugar, I know."

He remembered. Why couldn't she?

After filling the tank—and she suspected it hadn't needed much—he crossed in front of the hood to the brightly lit station. His overcoat swirled around his long lean legs, and a breeze ruffled his gleaming black hair.

He was successful, powerful... If not for love, why had he married her?

What kind of woman had she been before her abduction?

She opened her eyes and leaned forward in the seat to gaze into the rearview mirror. A woman with a pale face and wide frightened eyes stared back at her.

Slightly crooked nose. Chopped-up hair. She was no beauty, not now if she had ever been.

But beauty mattered little to her. Raising her son, being a good loving mother—that was all she cared about.

Not a man.

Not even her husband.

And although he claimed he'd spent six years searching for her, she didn't think he cared much, either.

But he had agreed to help her.

And right now, help was more important to her than love, than passion. Than any of her forgotten past.

Now if she could only forget that kiss. The one that had weakened her knees and threatened to make her faint as memories had loomed at the edge of her consciousness. So close.

Why did her body remember him so well when her mind did not? Her pulse beat faster in his presence, her breath shallower. Her body had known his intimately, as evidenced by their son, who looked so much like his father.

But after what she'd been through, after what a *man* had nearly done to her once, would she ever want to be intimate with one again?

A kiss was nothing.

Liar.

Somehow she knew that if he even gave her a chaste kiss on the cheek, passion would flare between them.

Lights flashed in the mirror, blinding her for a moment until she refocused. The headlamps were up high, and behind them gleamed the metal of a big pickup truck.

Then the beams flashed off. And she could see the driver, who stared back at her. Her breath caught in her throat, threatening to choke her.

The glow of the lights from the station illuminated the interior of the cab, shining off the pale blond, almost white hair of the driver.

And the white of his blind eye, which he closed in a wink.

Chapter Six

Using an elbow, Evan pushed open the door to the gas station and juggled two foam cups of scalding hot coffee. At the roar of an engine, he glanced up and saw a truck peel out of the lot, spewing gravel from the rear tires.

The familiarity of the noise caused him to jerk, and coffee oozed from under the lid and over his fingers, leaving a burnt trail. "Amanda!"

The station lights glinted off the windshield of the Viper, casting shadows in the interior. No blond hair gleamed, nor green eyes flashed. Had the bastard taken her right out from under him?

Evan tossed the cups down and raced toward the passenger's door, jerking at the handle. The lock held. When he pounded on the glass, Amanda rose up from where she had crouched on the floorboards. Tears shimmered in her enormous fear-widened eyes, and her hands shook as she struggled with the door.

"Evan!" She catapulted out of the car and into his arms. "It was him!"

He didn't want to believe it, but he knew she spoke the truth. And he cursed himself for leaving her alone and vulnerable. His arms tightened around her trembling body. "He's gone."

Parked in a corner of the lot was one of the bodyguards he had hired. The woman, Cullen Murphy's sister and an ex-cop, would have been there, would have acted if something outwardly threatening had happened. "What did he do, Amanda?"

She shuddered. "He winked."

The bastard was playing with her, taunting her. He wanted absolute power over her before he tortured and killed her. Evan got the message and read Weering's intent.

Maybe the evidence didn't exist to tie Weering to those other crimes, but Evan knew he had killed those victims. Only Amanda had survived, and Weering wouldn't let her live if he had a chance.

Evan couldn't give him that chance.

She jerked free of his arms. "You don't believe me. You don't think I saw him!"

He guided her back into the passenger's seat. "I believe you, Amanda. And now we have to get back on the road."

"To Christopher. We have to get Christopher before he tries…"

Evan rounded the hood and slid behind the wheel. "He won't. Our son is safe."

Our son.

He'd said the words. He'd accepted that he was a father, accepted the child he never thought he'd have with Amanda.

To calm her fears about her son, Evan punched in Royce's number.

"Everything okay?" the ex-agent said as he answered his phone.

Evan sighed into his cell. "What have you heard?"

"About Snake's murder. Be careful, man. That's one dangerous SOB."

"I know. How's the boy?"

"Good. He enjoyed our little adventure. I brought him home with me. He's had fun playing with Jeremy, but now he's tired. He wants his mom and he's been asking about you."

"Me?"

"I think he knows, Evan. You guys are going to have to tell him something." Royce chuckled. "And here he is."

Evan bit off a remark as the little boy came on the phone. "Hi," said the high-pitched voice.

He hadn't intended to speak to him and was totally unprepared for the wave of warmth that spread through his chest. "Hi, Christopher. Are you having fun?"

"Uh-huh. Is my mommy with you?" his son asked.

"Yes, she is." He glanced to the passenger's seat, relieved to see she had pulled herself together at the mention of her son's name.

She reached for the phone, but before Evan could hand it over, the little boy asked one more question. "Are you my daddy?"

In the background Royce's groan echoed the one Evan swallowed. But he could not lie, not to his son. "Yes, I am."

"Okay. Can I talk to my mommy now?"

With nerveless fingers, Evan passed the phone to her. Then, with an urge to get back on the road, he started the car and eased out of the station lot. He divided his time between watching for truck lights and watching Amanda.

Her face, animated as she told an obviously oft-repeated bedtime story to their son, had never been lovelier. Her full lips moved as she made silly noises and her eyes flashed with humor. But despite the show of bravado for Christopher, Evan sensed her fear. When she hung up after an emotional goodbye to their son, she confirmed his suspicion.

She blew out a ragged breath, her bangs dancing across her forehead. "You must think I'm such a coward, hiding like I was."

Evan glanced from the winding Lake Michigan coastal road, his gaze skimming over her pale face. Long curly lashes fluttered over those wide green eyes fighting back tears. "You have a damn good reason to be afraid. In fact, you'd be a fool if you weren't."

"I'm afraid of you, too."

That startled him. What did she know? "You are?"

"You told him."

He sighed. "He's a smart little kid. He asked and I couldn't lie to him."

"Why not?"

Good question.

Life would be much simpler if he had. But from the moment he'd met Amanda, life had been anything *but* simple for Evan. "I don't lie."

"So anything I ask you about the past, you'll tell me the truth?"

No matter how painful...

If she asked him again why he had married her, he'd tell her the truth.

"Yes."

"That scares me, too."

To his relief she asked no questions, and a tense silence filled the Viper. When he glanced her way again and again, he noticed she kept her eyes closed. But he didn't think she was asleep, for her hands were clenched so tightly in her lap that the tips of her nails had turned white while the beds were a deep red. Like blood.

Frustration had him pressing harder on the accelerator. He could do nothing to calm her fear of the dark—God knew she had a reason to be afraid—but he could get her to her son faster, could get her to the safety of his house in Winter Falls. Home.

"Amanda, it's not much farther."

"Good."

"We'll be there in less than an hour." If he kept pushing the speed limit.

Lights appeared in his rearview, closer than the distance at which Murphy had been following. In fact, he had not noticed Murphy's lights for some time now.

"Amanda, hand me the cell phone." She'd kept it on her lap after talking to their son.

The lights kept coming, gaining on the Viper despite their speed. As he eased into a curve, Evan accelerated and downshifted, counting on the tires gripping the asphalt. Gravel from the shoulder spewed up behind them.

"What's wrong?" Amanda asked as she held out the cell phone to him. With both hands locked on the steering wheel, he couldn't reach for it. She sat it on the console at his elbow. "Why are you going so fast now?"

Then she glanced back just as the vehicle, shining high beams into the Viper, edged closer. "Oh, my God, it's him, isn't it?"

Evan rounded the next curve, tires squealing. "I don't know."

But he wasn't taking any chances. If he slowed up to let the driver pass, he might wind up pushed off the coastal road by the jacked-up truck if it was Weering. Evan wanted to know if it was. In the next open stretch of dark highway, he eased his foot up some on the pedal.

Amanda's fingers clutched at the sleeve of his overcoat. "Why are you slowing down? Don't let him catch us!"

Evan glanced over and noted the paleness of her face, white but for the glow of the amber dashboard lights reflecting off her translucent skin. "You're safe, Amanda."

She shivered. "I thought you never lie."

"Amanda..."

The squeal of tires behind him brought his attention to his sideview mirror since the high beams in the rearview would blind him. As the two vehicles edged single file around another sharp curve, he caught a glimpse of the side of the one behind them. A pickup truck.

Amanda's breath caught. "It is him."

"Yeah, I'd bet it is."

Playing with them.

The truck jumped forward, front bumper nearly touching the rear one of the Viper. Such an action could force the sports car off the road. Evan couldn't allow that to happen. He downshifted and pressed on the accelerator and the clutch. The powerful car shot ahead, fishtailing around the next corner.

Evan gripped the wheel hard as the car lurched toward the gravel shoulder on the opposite side of the winding road. The shoulder gave way to steep rocky hillside, below which Lake Michigan glistened under a sprinkling of stars in the dark sky. Just as lights from an oncoming car appeared directly in front of him, he maneuvered the Viper back into the right lane.

In his mirror he spied the truck, which didn't steer as easily back to the right. Sparks flew into the night as the front fender of the pickup scraped the car going south. The screech of metal grinding against metal rose above the purr of the Viper's engine.

"Call 911!" he shouted as he witnessed the other car slide off the shoulder.

With a shaking hand Amanda grabbed up the phone and punched in the number. "There's been an acc—someone's forced a car off the road—"

"On old 131," Evan supplied when she floundered, her voice quavering with fear. Would theirs be the next vehicle forced from the road? Not if Evan could control it. And there wasn't much he didn't at least try to control…including his own baser instincts.

He downshifted and slammed on the brakes, forcing the Viper into a U-turn. "I have to make sure those people are all right, Amanda. The police might not get here in time."

In time for any of them.

WHEN EVAN CUT THE ENGINE, silence reigned. No sound. Not even the chirp of a cricket broke the stillness of the night. Then a breath shuddered out of Amanda, as fear gripped her. "Evan…"

"I have to check on those people, Amanda." He reached for the handle of his door, but she caught his arm.

"He's out there!"

Evan's dark eyes shone in the dim lights from the dashboard. He'd left the key turned in the ignition, the headlamps burning holes in the darkness on the shoulder of the curving road. Would that feeble light be enough to find the wreckage? Amanda doubted it.

"He might be. Or he might be long gone, Amanda. But I'm not taking that chance. You're going with me."

Except for those circles of light, darkness engulfed the small car. She shivered. "I can't…"

But then the memory of being alone while he'd gone into the station flashed through her mind. An image of her cowering on the floorboards until he'd returned. Knowing that Weering could have taken her at any time…

She reached for the handle. "Okay."

Beneath the swinging door, darkness and empty air reigned. Stones skittered down the steep hillside. "Evan—"

But he'd already stepped out of the car. Then he was on her side, lifting her down from her seat, his arms strong and reassuring as he set her on her feet. He kept her sheltered against his side, his arm anchored tight around her, as they scrambled over rocks and scraggly bushes lining the hillside. Darkness hiding the sharp rocks and thorny bushes, as it probably hid other dangers.

Weering.

Where was he? Did he lurk in the darkness waiting for an opportunity to attack again?

Amanda shivered even though Evan shielded her from the cold night wind whipping off the lake. Waves crashed beneath them, frothing on the shore. But before the water, suspended upside down, was the wreckage of the car. Its smashed lights bored into the ground beneath it, glancing off stones and weeds and broken glass from the shattered windshield.

And more than those crashing waves broke the stillness of the night. Screams.

Shame over her selfishness lowered Amanda's head. She hadn't wanted to stop. She had been too scared of what might happen to her. But these people…they had done nothing to deserve this pain. All they had done was travel the same road where a madman stalked his victim. Her.

"Oh, my God." And she prayed for them. "You have to help them!"

She never doubted that Evan could.

His deep voice rumbled out of the darkness. "Stay here."

"But—" Again selfish fear paralyzed her. She didn't want to be left alone, didn't want him to leave her, even though she knew those people were in more immediate danger than she was.

Clinging heavy to the mist off the lake was the odor of gasoline as it wafted from the wreckage. "You can't get any closer," Evan warned her, his dark gaze glittering in the night sky as he leaned close.

Then his head lifted and he tensed. Noises drifted down from above. The grind of a motor but no sirens, nothing to indicate it was the help she'd called. Then a dark shadow scrambled down the hill toward them.

Amanda shuddered and drew closer to Evan. "Murphy?" he called out.

"Yeah," a female voice grunted, and when the woman neared, Amanda recognized her.

"I saw you today. At the pawnshop…" And outside the D.A.'s office. She turned back to Evan. "You've had someone following me."

"And doing a bad job of it," the woman admitted. "I'm sorry he got past me. You're okay?" She peered around them to the wreckage. "Oh, my God!"

"I'm going to see what I can do to help," Evan said. "We've called the police. They should be on their way. Watch her."

Because *he* might still be out there. Somewhere in the darkness she feared so much. Waiting for her.

AMANDA BREATHED a sigh of relief a couple of hours later when they reached Evan's home in Winter Falls. Although Evan had shut the front door and reengaged his security system, she didn't consider those measures enough to protect her. She didn't think anything could protect her, but this one man who she couldn't remember seemed to be her best hope.

A muscle twitched in his clenched jaw and his dark eyes swirled with anger. Not at her. She knew where it was directed—at Weering.

She followed his long strides down a wide hallway to where the house opened up. Through skylights in the ceiling of the two-story great room, stars twinkled.

And the rear wall of glass reflected those same stars off the surface of Lake Michigan far below the cliff into which the house was built.

A fortress. Impenetrable. And with slate floors, stainless-steel stairwell and stark white walls, cold.

Some might say the house reflected the man, but she wouldn't. She had no memory of him on which to base her opinion, but that fire, that anger, burned deep in his eyes, in his soul.

"You hired someone to follow me," Amanda stated. A woman who could go everywhere she went without raising suspicion. Bathrooms. Changing rooms. Evan Quade was the kind of man who left nothing to chance.

"She's from a security firm—they're supposed to be the best."

She shivered. Maybe the best wasn't enough, not against a madman. "He forced her off the road so he could pass and get to us. She's lucky she wasn't hurt."

"And those people in the other car are going to be all right," she said, not knowing if he needed reassurance, but knowing that *she* did. "You got to them in time."

But their frightened screams from the wreckage still echoed in her head.

Evan offered her no reassurance now. After that one time in the car outside the gas station, he had never again promised that she was safe. While William Weering roamed free, she would find no security.

"He knocked them off the road and just drove off," she said, the horror washing over her again as it had when she'd seen that car, headlights boring into the ground as the crumpled vehicle lay upside down on the rocky hillside leading down to the water.

Despite the strong gasoline fumes, Evan had scrambled in the dark, over the rocks, down to the car. He had never let Amanda close enough to the accident, though, to see what he saw. What had made him so grim. He had performed first aid until the fire-rescue crew, ambulance and police had arrived.

"What did you expect him to do?" he asked, pushing a hand through his already tousled black hair as he stood near that wall of glass, staring at the water below.

"Come back and kill us." Every minute on that hillside had been pure agony for her despite the presence of her armed bodyguard.

He'd been there. Watching. She knew it.

Evan sighed. "Too easy. Too damn easy."

She shuddered. "What are you saying?"

When he turned back toward her, the anger burned brighter in his dark eyes. "He's playing with you, Amanda. Taunting you."

"He wants me to suffer." She wrapped her arms tight around herself, holding in the tremors of fear. "If he wants to hurt me the most, he'll hurt my child. That's why we need to get Christopher tonight."

"It's too late. You know he's sleeping. And if Weering is following *you,* he's safe where he's at."

Safer away from her than with her. That's what Evan was saying. The truth of that shattered her more than any of the madman's threats. Her very presence endangered her child. "I can't abandon my child. I'm the only parent he knows," she argued desperately.

Evan winced. "I don't expect you to abandon him, Amanda. Just let him sleep tonight." The unspoken *at Royce's, away from you,* hung between them.

"I'm sorry." She sighed, frustration, fear and exhaustion fraying her nerves. "You really didn't know that I—that I was pregnant before I…"

"Left me?" He turned away from her again, shrugging out of his overcoat, stained now with the blood of the accident victims.

Along with not remembering the past, she couldn't imagine being with this man, let alone leaving him. Except for that flicker of recognition with his kiss and the ensuing conflagration of passion.

She licked dry lips, lips that still bore the slight flavor of his rich kiss. "I don't know…"

He chuckled, but no laugh lines wrinkled in his face. Was he a man without humor in his life? From the starkness of his house, one might conclude that he had nothing in his life.

Since she left? A small part of her rejoiced in that thought, selfish as it was. Another mourned.

"You don't believe it. You still don't accept that you are my wife," he said.

If he refused to lie, so would she. "No, I don't completely accept it. I know you probably have proof, but I can't remember. I can't believe it unless I can remember."

He dragged in a quick breath. "I dumped our coffee earlier. Do you still want some?"

She nodded, knowing that with or without the influence of caffeine, sleep would prove unattainable for her. "Yes."

"The pot's on the counter, beans and grinder in the

drawer below it.'' He gestured toward the kitchen, which was in a corner of the great room, separated from it only by a long granite island.

She stiffened over his lack of manners to a guest. But then, *was* she a guest? If she could believe him, she was his wife. So even though she had never lived here, didn't that make this house as much hers as his? She glanced around the deep gray slate floors and unadorned walls and shuddered. This house would *never* be hers.

''Fine, I'll make the coffee,'' she said after a moment.

He hadn't waited for her acquiescence though as he'd already stridden back down the hall to the French doors that opened off of it and into a den.

Business.

Why did she assume that? And why did the thought fill her with resentment?

Dizzy, she swayed on her feet, gripping at the granite counter to avoid crumpling to the hard floor. Tired. That was all. Fatigue and stress inevitably brought on the headaches and the episodes of dizziness.

Maybe coffee would help. Forcing her hands to steady, she measured out beans into the grinder, breathing in the rich aroma. In minutes she had set the pot to brew, and the scent increased. Seductively rich. Like Evan.

And she was alone with him. And despite the starkness of their surroundings, this was even more intimate than the close confines of his sports car. This was his home.

Would she ever be able to return to hers? To the little house partially paid for by the watch found on her battered body after the attack. But that tiny bungalow had never felt like home.

No more than this place.

"Did I ever live here?" she asked, sensing his presence by the enticing scent of his cologne and the power of his personality. She glanced over her shoulder to where he leaned against the granite island across from her.

"No. I told you before that you never really had a home."

"Where'd I grow up?"

"London, Paris, Rome, Milan…in some of the finest hotel suites in those magnificent cities—that's what you told me. Never seemed to bother you."

"What did bother me back then?"

"Maybe me. I don't know."

"So that's why I left. Not because I didn't want a child." That reason still gnawed at her. She couldn't imagine not wanting Christopher.

His gaze hardened.

She dragged in a quick breath, not wanting to travel down a painful road again tonight. He had told her already that it was because he'd wanted children and she hadn't. What kind of woman had she been?

"So where are my parents now?"

"Probably in one of those cities. And they've moved into the double digits on marriages now."

"Combined?"

"Each."

She shivered, not able to accept that she came from people like the ones he described. "Do they…have they…"

"Searched for you?"

She nodded.

He shrugged, but his dark eyes softened with sympathy. "You and your father had a fight before you left. You quit working for him. He's a fashion designer. He was furious and disowned you."

And being a man who could cut off his association with wife after wife, he'd had no problem cutting off contact with a daughter. Had he not loved her at all? Had he only loved what she'd done for his business? Emptiness yawned within Amanda until an image of Christopher racing off the school bus and into her arms flashed through her mind.

"And my mother?" Wasn't the bond between a mother and child unbreakable, like hers with Christopher?

He chuckled. "Mother? You've never been able to call her that. When you were young, nannies raised you. She had little contact with you, ever. But you went to her after you left me, or you went to her estate outside Chicago anyway. That's where you were last seen."

And sometime after that she'd fallen into the clutches of a madman. She couldn't think about that, not now, not when night wrapped around the house.

"You're not painting a very pretty picture of the past." *My past.* But she couldn't claim it, not when she couldn't remember it.

"I don't think you thought that back then. It was all you knew."

And now that she was a mother, she knew differently. She knew the unsurpassed joy of the first time Christopher had called her mama. She couldn't imagine never wanting that. She couldn't imagine any of the past. And did she even want to try? Was there anything worth remembering?

Besides him.

Evan would be worth it. Or would he? Would the memories only bring more pain?

Her headache hammered at her, and she winced under the pressure.

"Do you want to remember, Amanda?" His dark eyes stared at her, maybe into her, since his question was so perceptive.

"I don't know." She turned back to the pot mounted under the white cabinet. "Coffee's done."

Her stomach flipped at the thought of drinking any now, so late at night. But the thought of closing her eyes to sleep summoned other images, images from Snake Timmer's apartment. She shivered.

"A cup will warm you up," Evan advised.

What warmed her up was his lean length pressing against her back as he reached into the cupboard above her head. Then he set down a coffee mug on the counter on either side of her, his arms remaining in a loose embrace around her.

She struggled with the urge to turn in his arms and lay her cheek against his strong chest. She had already laid her troubles on the broad shoulders of this stranger. Her husband?

His breath shuddered out, warm against her cheek as he dipped his head close to her ear. "Why is it so hard to accept that you are my wife?"

Something in his voice compelled her to tip back her head and meet his tortured gaze. Why did it matter so much to him that she couldn't remember him? Had he cared about her?

She couldn't help but feel sorry for him if he had. *That* woman was dead to him. And she doubted she would ever be resurrected, in memory or spirit.

"I don't know." She sighed, at a loss. "There's so much I don't know."

"I can help you."

She turned then, to stroke her hand along his hard jaw. The stubble of his five-o'clock shadow tickled her fingertips, sending a tingling sensation up her arm. "You're helping me already. And I've never thanked you. You're putting your life on the line for me."

She wanted to take it personally, wanted to believe it had something to do with her; with the woman she had been and the one she was now. But she'd seen his response to strangers in trouble. And that's all she was to him. A stranger.

He caught her hand, pulling it away from his face but not releasing it. His fingers wove through hers. "Amanda, I don't see it like that."

"You told me that I'm in danger. You can't deny that. And just by being with me, you're in danger, too."

His eyes darkened as he shuttered whatever emotion flickered through them. She didn't know why he bothered, she couldn't read him anyway. "Amanda…"

"You had the faster car tonight. That's the only reason we didn't wind up like those poor people, turned upside down. We could have died. Both of us." Had that happened, they would have orphaned Christopher. Her breath caught as she thought of her son raised by anyone but her. Strangers who wouldn't love him as she did.

A thunderous look flashed in Evan's eyes. "He didn't want to run us off the road, Amanda."

She shuddered, and he used their linked hands to pull her into his arms. Her cheek rested against his shoulder, tears spilling from her eyes onto his silk shirt. "You think he's playing with us, taunting us?"

"Running you off the road is too impersonal. It's not part of his plan."

Torturing her was. Raping her. Killing her. Slowly. Painfully. As he'd killed his ex-cell mate.

"I'm so scared, Evan." The confession tumbled out with a wretched sob.

His broad hand stroked over her back in a warm caress. "You're safe here."

Safe from Weering? She doubted it. She also doubted that, despite her memory loss, she was safe from the past.

"Come on," Evan finally said. "Pour the coffee and come with me into the living room. I have something that'll take your mind off…everything."

She appreciated his effort, but she knew nothing would take her mind off everything. Nothing but losing it again.

But because she didn't want to be alone or try to sleep, she poured the coffee and handed him a mug. Then after she'd added cream and sugar to hers, she followed him back into the great room.

Across a granite slab of a coffee table he had dropped some albums. What he'd retrieved from the den?

"What are these?" she asked as she settled beside him onto the supple leather sofa and reached toward one of the albums.

"Our wedding albums."

She regretted the sip of coffee she'd taken when it scalded her throat as she choked on it. She jerked her hand away from the closest book. "I don't think this is the time to…"

Resurrect the past? To resurrect Amanda Quade? She knew neither was possible, so why try? Why put them both through the disappointment and pain?

"Just look, Amanda. What can it hurt?" he gently prodded.

A lot.

"You still don't believe me. I see it in your eyes, so look at the proof. Look at yourself back then."

He flipped over a book bound in varnished maple. On the top cover, a heart had been carved out of the wood, and in the middle stood a smiling couple. A younger happy Evan had his arm wrapped around a glowing young blonde. Hair flowed past her shoulders and around the square bodice of a radiantly white wedding gown. A flirtatious smile tipped up the woman's full lips, and pure happiness filled her green eyes as she gazed up at her husband.

Jealousy flashed through Amanda over the way the woman looked at Evan, over the proprietary way she leaned into his arms. Then she realized this woman was supposed to be her.

"No, it doesn't even look like me. You've made a mistake." She edged away, reaching with trembling hands for her coffee cup.

What would he do now? Would he withdraw his offer of protection since she was obviously *not* his wife?

He chuckled softly.

"Amanda, look closer. It's you. Look beyond the hair and clothes."

Although pain throbbed behind her eyes, she glanced again. He opened the book, flashing other photos in front of her. More of the same smiling care-free couple.

Until he thumbed to a candid shot, later in the book, she didn't believe it was her. But in this photo, the woman gazed pensively across a garden, yearning.

As *she* yearned.

All those years ago that woman had had everything. Or had she? What had she yearned for then?

Now Amanda yearned for security.

Pain throbbed at her temples and pounded in her head. "I'm tired."

"I can show you to the guest room."

She caught his wrist as he leaned forward to place the album back on the table. "No, let me look."

With trembling fingers she flipped through those pages, staring at people she didn't recognize, wondering who they were, who she was.

Evan sat stiffly beside her, sipping coffee and studying her with those dark eyes so like her son's. Like *his* son's.

They had been married. In the back of the album the marriage certificate bore both of their names. His. And the one he'd told her had been hers.

Although she began to believe him, she didn't know what it would change. She'd never again be the woman he had married. If William Weering III had his way, she wouldn't even *be* much longer.

While going through the albums, she must have dozed off because she awoke to sunlight pouring through the two-story windows. Squinting against the brightness, she glanced around her and found Evan still asleep, slouched beside her. She had curled up against him, her head resting on his broad shoulder.

She must have snuggled up to him for safety. Not because this man inexplicably drew her to him. And certainly not because she still looked at him as the woman in the album had all those years ago.

He offered protection to her, nothing more. Not love. And she was glad, relieved. Because love wasn't something she could either return or accept.

Then she realized more than the sunlight had awakened her. Near the front door, something rattled, and any sense of safety she'd felt in Evan's arms fled.

Someone was breaking into his fortress.

Chapter Seven

Evan jolted to full wakefulness, conscious of the sudden tension in Amanda's body. When she had fallen asleep on him earlier, she'd been relaxed, vulnerable. Her soft hair had tickled his throat, and the scent of her peaches-and-cream shampoo had filled his senses. "What's go—"

"He's at the door, Evan! He's found us!"

He shook off the last vestiges of sleep and the passion for her that had clouded his mind. "What! He couldn't get inside the gates."

The doorknob rattled, but before he could rush the intruder, a female voice called out, "Mr. Quade? Evan?"

Recognizing the voice, Evan pulled Amanda back against his side. "It's fine. It's just my secretary," he soothed as the front door opened.

The woman gasped as she entered the great room. "Mr. Quade. I'm sorry. I should have rung the bell."

He nodded and narrowed his eyes at her boldness. "Or waited at the office to hear from me. I would have called you later this morning."

Color flushed her usually pale face, and she pushed

lank blond hair behind her ear with a trembling hand. "I'm sorry. It's just that it's early. Since you gave me the code, I didn't think it'd be an issue if I just dropped these contracts off for you. You've been waiting for the lawyer to send them."

Her gaze slid from his and settled on Amanda. "I know they're important," she added, her expression showing her distaste with Evan's guest.

Irritated with his secretary's audacity, he didn't see fit to make introductions. He had only given her the security code for when he was gone, not for when he was home. And he had made that clear to her. She could come by the house, drop mail, water plants as part of her generous salary. But to intrude when he was home…

"Ms. Moore, we'll discuss this another time, at the office." With an effort, he disengaged himself from Amanda and rose from the sofa.

Rumpled from sleep and flushed with embarrassment, Amanda was adorable, something he never would have considered her six years ago. Beautiful— yes. Alluring—absolutely. But not adorable. He would never have suspected he would be so drawn to adorable, yet she attracted him more now than she ever had.

Stiffness attacked his joints and other muscles from being tangled up with his wife, sleeping on the couch. He'd wanted to do more than sleep. But he knew she didn't need him like that. She only needed his protection.

He ran his hand along his prickly jaw and over his tousled hair as he crossed the sun-drenched great

If offer card is missing write to: The Harlequin Reader Service, 3010 Walden Ave., P.O. Box 1867, Buffalo, NY 14240-1867

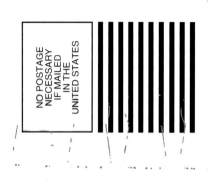

NO POSTAGE
NECESSARY
IF MAILED
IN THE
UNITED STATES

BUSINESS REPLY MAIL

FIRST-CLASS MAIL   PERMIT NO. 717-003   BUFFALO, NY

POSTAGE WILL BE PAID BY ADDRESSEE

HARLEQUIN READER SERVICE
3010 WALDEN AVE
PO BOX 1867
BUFFALO NY 14240-9952

Do You Have the LUCKY KEY?

PLAY THE
Lucky Key Game

and you can get

Scratch the gold areas with a coin. Then check below to see the books and gift you can get!

FREE BOOKS and a FREE GIFT!

YES! I have scratched off the gold areas. Please send me the **2 FREE BOOKS** and **GIFT** for which I qualify. I understand I am under no obligation to purchase any books, as explained on the back of this card.

382 HDL DVGA   182 HDL DVGQ

FIRST NAME	LAST NAME

ADDRESS

APT.#	CITY

STATE / PROV.	ZIP/POSTAL CODE

2 free books plus a free gift   1 free book

2 free books   Try Again!

Visit us online at
www.eHarlequin.com

DETACH AND MAIL CARD TODAY!

(H-I-02/04)

room. He needed a shower. After sleeping platonically next to Amanda, probably a cold one.

"Let me show you out," he said to the young woman, who stood yet at the end of the entrance hall.

She nodded. "Of course, you will be into the office later."

"Later doesn't necessarily mean today. Marshall can handle everything that comes up, just as he has been." His vice president was very capable. "And if you get in a real jam, call Sarah. She still has more business sense than she'll admit to."

He chuckled over his former business partner's adverseness to the company that had made them both richer, through her investment and his management.

But his humor quickly fled, replaced by the emptiness he usually felt, but for those few hours when Amanda had slept in his arms.

"That's her." Cynthia Moore hissed the words at him, her thin lips pursed with distaste.

His gaze narrowed and skimmed over the tall skinny blonde. Cynthia yanked an expander file from under her arm and held it out to him.

"Here are the papers from the divorce lawyer. He said you don't need her signature, but since she's here…"

Cynthia Moore was more than a secretary, she was an assistant. But *only* a business assistant, which she sometimes forgot. His personal life was *not* her responsibility.

He shook his head and curled his hands into fists, refusing to accept the folder. "Take it back to the office. I'm not dealing with this now. And I'm not discussing it with you. Ask Marshall what he needs help with.''

Color flushed her face again and she chewed at her lip. ''But when are you coming in?''

''When I come in.''

As she passed through the door he held open for her, she opened her mouth, but he shook his head. If she pushed him any further with her nosiness…

She closed her mouth just as he closed the door behind her. He wouldn't risk saying anything more, anything that might hurt her. She had been a hard-working loyal employee for many years. Although she'd overstepped the boundaries, he didn't want to make a scene.

When he did go into the office, however, he'd remind her of those boundaries and that he needed her respect.

Evan found Amanda in the kitchen brewing more coffee. Her trembling hands scattered grounds across the granite counter. ''Relax, Amanda, it wasn't him.''

''Not this time.''

''He can't get past the gates, Amanda,'' he assured her. ''There's one at the street and another down at the beach entrance. This is a very safe place.''

When she remained silent, he continued, ''I increased security when a friend was staying here this past spring. Someone tried to kidnap her son from this house.''

She shuddered. ''But they didn't?''

''Yes, but not then.'' Seeing Amanda's expression, he added, ''He's fine. He and his mother are both fine. And it was a lesson to me.''

She studied him for a while before she asked,

"You care about this friend who stayed here? Care enough to increase security for her?"

"For the remainder of her stay, yes."

"Do you miss her?"

His mind must not have been fully awake yet because he couldn't understand the line of her questioning. "I didn't stay here with her. I stayed at an apartment in Traverse City. She is just a friend. She's Royce Graham's wife."

She sighed, a sigh of relief or pity, he had no idea which. "And you keep the security to keep other people from getting in?"

Now he understood. And apparently, so did she. They weren't talking about the house anymore. She'd surmised what other people had accused him of—locking himself and his feelings away. Maybe it was only fair to warn her. "Yes, I do."

"Your secretary who's just a secretary. She needs to know that."

EVEN AS SHE RODE next to Evan in his sports car an hour later, Amanda couldn't believe she'd said what she said. *She needs to know that.* Like a jealous wife.

She had no reason to be jealous of a husband she couldn't remember and didn't want. She *needed* him now…for protection. Only. No other reason.

She dragged in a deep breath, not sure if her thoughts had made her nervous or riding in his sports car again had. Memories of the night before washed over her. The high beams bearing down on them as Evan increased speed and maneuvered around hairpin curves.

If not for his skillful driving, surely they would

have crashed and tumbled into the lake, might still be in the frigid water. Dead.

"This morning you checked on the people from last night's accident?" She could still hear their screams from the wreckage, still see Evan's coat covered with blood from Weering's innocent victims.

He nodded, his gaze locked on the road. "The hospital said they're in stable condition."

"So that's good." But she wondered who else would get hurt because of her. Because a madman was after her. She prayed not her son, and not Evan.

"We're almost to Royce and Sarah's," he said, probably sensing her impatience to see her little boy.

"We've never been apart, Christopher and I, not this long. Last night was hard for me, in more ways than one."

He groaned, and she barely caught his mumbled words. "Me, too."

What had been hard for him? Showing her photo albums and getting no reaction? What had he expected?

The memory of the kiss he'd given her in River City flashed through her mind, and heat flashed through her body. Had he expected her to act like a wife?

But she barely resembled that poised and perfectly groomed woman he had married. Surely he didn't feel anything for her but pity and a sense of responsibility?

She didn't want his pity, but in just a couple of days, she had come to rely on his overdeveloped sense of responsibility. Last night it had surely saved her life and undoubtedly the lives of those people from the wreck.

"It's so early we'll probably get there before he wakes up," Evan said.

She nodded and turned to the window to fight her tears without falling under the scrutiny of his dark gaze. All she could do was pray that Evan was right and Weering had no plans to hurt her child.

If Christopher were in danger because of her, she would have to entrust his care to others, to people who could keep him safe. Instead of endangering him.

"We're here." The sports car slowed as Evan downshifted near a wrought-iron fence. Brick pillars separated a gate from the fence. He opened his window, leaning out to press numbers on a security pad.

Conscious of other people's privacy, Amanda glanced away. In the woods across the street from them, she spied some movement. A shadow separated from the tree trunks. Sunlight funneled through the barren branches and reflected off a head of pale blond hair.

"Evan!"

The gates started to slide open and she clutched at his arm. "No! He's right over there."

Evan whipped around in his seat. "Where?"

"In the woods."

He propelled the car through the half-open gates, jerking to a halt just inside the grounds. "Run up to the house, Amanda."

She tightened her grip on the sleeve of his leather jacket, but he opened the door and slipped free. "Where are you going?"

"After him." And he dashed through the gates just

as they closed, shutting her safely inside and him outside with a killer.

She threw open the passenger door and vaulted out of the car, running to the gate. "Evan! Come back!"

Through the wrought-iron spires, she watched him charge across the street and wade into the scraggly undergrowth of the woods. Wrapping her fingers around the iron, she held on and held out hope that he would return, screaming, "Evan!"

If he could hear her, he ignored her urgency and slipped deeper into the woods and out of her sight. She whirled around, her gaze encountering the house, a massive structure of fieldstone and cedar. Shoes pounding on the cement drive, she ran for the front door. Then she alternated jabbing at the bell and hammering at the solid oak.

A shadow shifted behind the stained-glass side window, and the door opened. "Amanda?" Royce Graham blinked sleep from his bleary eyes.

"Mr. Graham, Royce! You have to find him, stop him!"

"What? Who? Weering's here?"

She nodded, fear choking her voice.

The ex-FBI agent pulled her into the house and behind him, putting himself between her and outside. "And Evan?"

"He went after him. They're in the woods across the street."

Royce slammed the exterior door, then disappeared through an archway off the hall.

"Royce! You have to help him!"

From somewhere deeper inside the house, a child's voice rang out, "Mommy!"

Little feet pounded on the hardwood, thundering down the hall. "Mommy!"

She caught up her boy in trembling arms. "Baby. Oh, baby, thank God you're safe."

Tears burned her eyes, but she blinked them back just in time to see The Tracker return, tucking a gun into the waistband of his jeans.

"I'm not a baby," her little boy protested as he burrowed his sleepy face into her neck.

Over his dark curly head, she caught the approach of a red-haired woman and gangly teenager from the direction from which Christopher had catapulted. The woman, tall and slim, wore silk pajamas, and although her hair was tousled, she still looked elegant, poised. Everything Amanda was not, especially as fear for Evan's safety had her knees knocking.

"Call Dylan," Royce told the woman. "Evan went after the bas—" With a glance at Christopher, he cut off the word. "In the woods across the street."

Then one hand on the butt of the gun at his waist, he pulled open the door.

"Dad!" the teenager protested.

The woman's fingers, tapered with long polished nails, wrapped around the boy's arm. "This is what he does, Jeremy. He'll come back. He always comes back."

Over his shoulder Royce shot the woman a look so full of love that he needed no words to express what was in his heart. Everyone could see it. And the look included his son. Then he closed the door behind his back, rushing off to face the danger with Evan.

Maybe Royce always returned, but Amanda had no guarantees about Evan. He wasn't an ex-FBI agent.

All she knew about this man she was married to was that he ran a business. And like everything he did—driving a car, gaining her trust—Amanda imagined he did it well.

But he didn't face down deranged killers. Except for the fire escape. And the road incident the night before. Since finding her, he had been in danger, had willingly put himself between it and her.

From the archway the woman's voice drifted, "Dylan, Evan and Royce are tracking the killer across the street from our house. Hurry!"

"Uncle Dylan is the sheriff," the teenage boy told her. "He'll get here fast. He'll help them. They'll be fine." Despite his words of encouragement, his voice shook.

Christopher lifted his head from her shoulder and smiled at the teenager, his dark eyes warm with affection. "Jeremy…"

"Thank you," she said, grateful for his sincere assurance to her and kindness to her son.

The older boy blushed, a tide of red rising into his fair skin to the roots of his golden-blond hair. "I didn't do anything. My dad and Evan—"

She shook her head. "No, you did."

The woman reappeared in the hall, almost as if she were a red-haired apparition, her movements were so fluid. "He's coming. They'll be fine. Let's go into the kitchen. I think I have some of those cookies left from yesterday unless you boys ate them all."

"We left some for this morning, Mom." The boy

forced a grin and winked at Christopher. "You up for some more chocolate chips, little buddy?"

Christopher nodded. "Uh-huh. Those are good." Then he glanced guiltily into Amanda's face. "Yours are, too, Mommy." His little voice broke. "I missed you last night." He pressed a quick kiss against her cheek. "But I had fun."

He scrambled down from her arms and tugged on Jeremy's hand, heading farther into the house, undoubtedly to those cookies.

Amanda's arms hung at her sides, limp without the weight of her boy. Empty. Her guilt clawed its way free and poured out of her. "He was right outside your house. I'm so sorry. So sorry. I should have stayed in River City. I never should have come here. I put you and your family in danger. I'm so sorry."

A silk-covered arm wrapped around her shuddering shoulders. "You haven't put anyone in danger. This is not your fault, Amanda. You're the victim."

She cringed, hating that term, hating how helpless she felt again because of William Weering III.

"I'm Sarah," the woman said. "I don't think we've been introduced."

But she knew who Amanda was, probably knew more than Amanda did about Mrs. Evan Quade.

"Thank you for taking care of my son last night," Amanda said.

Sarah's laugh rang out like the tinkling music of wind chimes. "He's a delight."

"He's a very busy little boy."

"I understand—I raised one myself." The woman

sighed and her arm lightly squeezed Amanda's shoulders. "For a while all by myself."

"Royce—" She stopped herself from a probing question that she had no right to ask. These people were Evan's friends, not hers.

Sarah's smile flowed into her words, "Royce adopted Jeremy when we got married last summer."

Newlyweds. And she'd let him go off chasing a killer, all the while maintaining her elegant poise. Meanwhile Amanda fell apart inside with worry for Evan.

But then Sarah didn't know William Weering III, didn't know evil as intimately as Amanda did.

"Come with me, Amanda. We'll see if those boys saved us some cookies and brew some coffee to go along…"

Not wanting to be rude, Amanda nevertheless shifted from under the woman's arm and turned toward the front door. Sunlight filtered through the stained glass, splashing puddles of color onto the hardwood floor. "I—I need to know that they're all right."

That Evan was all right.

"They'll be fine." The woman's voice didn't shake when she repeated her son's words. She brooked no argument, would allow nothing less than the well-being of their men.

Their men? Was Evan hers?

When he had expertly maneuvered the car around those hairpin turns the night before, she'd noted more than his grip on the steering wheel. She'd noted that he still wore his wedding ring. The ring one of those photos in the album had showed her placing on his finger. Her ring.

Despite the warmth of the sunlight she shivered in her Thinsulate jacket. "Before Royce headed out, Evan was out there with that killer. Alone. No weapon."

He hadn't had Royce's gun. Hadn't had the safety of a faster car and knowledge of the road.

She had missed the pad of the teenager's bare feet on the floor, so his snort startled her as it announced his presence. "*Evan* is a weapon, Mrs. Quade."

Mrs. Quade. After nearly six years of being Amanda Smith, she doubted she would ever get used to being called another name, a stranger's name.

"What do you mean?"

"He's a ninth-degree black belt. Don't you remember?"

"Jeremy." Sarah's voice censored without the lecture.

"I'm sorry," he said, not a bit sheepishly, with more directness than she had seen in most adults. "I didn't think."

How many didn't think, or doubted her amnesia? How many thought she'd kept Evan's son from him by choice rather than ignorance of the boy's father's existence?

These were his friends. Wouldn't they rally around him and look on her with suspicion and resentment?

But she could still feel the weight of Sarah's supportive arm around her shoulders. Could feel the warmth of Jeremy's reassurance. These were good people. And she'd brought them nothing but trouble.

She furiously blinked back tears.

"I started the coffee, Mom," Jeremy said. "Rich like you like it."

"Did you sneak some?" she teased.

He laughed with unabashed guilt. "Oh, yeah."

"It'll stunt your growth."

Their lighthearted banter grated on Amanda's overwrought nerves, inducing a scream that she swallowed hard. But she couldn't stop the flow of her fear.

"I don't care what he knows about martial arts. That skill won't help him against a knife."

Behind her eyes flashed the image of Snake lying on the floor of his apartment, bleeding out of his empty eye sockets. Her knees trembled, threatening to give. But she wouldn't faint. She wouldn't even acknowledge the throb at her temples and the base of her once-broken skull.

Jeremy's fingers closed over her hand, squeezing. "Yes, it will, Mrs. Quade. He can disarm a man with a knife with little or no effort."

No effort.

She flashed back to Snake's apartment again, to the scene on the fire escape where the black-clothed figure had swung the knife at him and Evan had kicked it away.

Hope flickered to life, dispelling some of the chilling fear. "You're right. I saw him do that."

"You did?" Awe deepened the teenager's voice.

"Evan's gotta help me get up to my purple belt. He's so good."

Good at driving. Good at fighting off knife-wielding killers. But there was one weapon that Amanda didn't think he could fight off.

A gun.

She had no more than formed the thought when a shot rang out, rattling the windows of the house and the people waiting inside for news of the well-being of their loved ones.

Did she love Evan? Had she remembered that? Too late?

Chapter Eight

Evan brushed brambles from the legs of his pants while he kept his gaze trained on where Amanda stood inside the gate. He and Royce had just emerged from the woods after hearing Dylan's gunshots when Amanda erupted from the house with Jeremy and Sarah, all frenzied.

He understood Jeremy's and Sarah's concern for Royce—they loved him. But why had Amanda been so worried? Had she remembered anything? Did she care about him?

Reaching through the wrought-iron spires, Sarah slapped Dylan's shoulder before turning for the house. She'd already sent Jeremy back inside to make sure Christopher had not engorged himself with cookies. "You scared us half to death!" she admonished him over her shoulder.

Us?

Dylan defended his actions, shouting after her, "I wanted these headstrong fools out of the woods, and I knew gunfire would send them running...straight to it. Damn it! I'm the sheriff. This is my job. Neither of you should have gone after him alone!"

"Dylan." Royce tucked his weapon back into the waistband of his jeans and opened the gate with a few strokes on the security pad. "I was prepared."

That left just him.

Evan and the sheriff followed the ex-agent onto his estate, closing the gate behind them. Glancing across the street, Evan scanned the woods again, searching for any movement.

Anything.

Dylan cleared his throat, his blue gaze boring into Evan. "What the hell were you thinking?"

He hadn't been thinking. He'd acted in defense of his family, and he'd do it again in a minute. "What progress are you making on finding this killer?"

Even though she had turned away from them, Evan caught Amanda's flinch. He wanted to drag her under his arm, offer her comfort, but he didn't know if she wanted that now. She had turned toward the garage in the rear of the house, where a member of Murphy Security had parked her van.

Was she thinking of leaving? That she'd be safer on her own than with him?

Dylan sighed. "No trace, Evan. Nobody's seen the truck you described. Nobody's seen a man fitting that pretty unique description anywhere around Winter Falls."

"I saw him!" Amanda's voice quivered with fear.

Dylan turned toward her, his eyes narrowed. "What did you see, Mrs. Quade?"

"I—I saw his hair."

"Hair?"

"In the trees, he might have been hiding behind one, but I saw the sun shine off his hair."

Dylan nodded and turned to Evan, a question in his eyes. "Did you see him?"

Evan shook his head and Amanda gasped.

"You didn't see him?" she asked.

He fought a frustrated sigh as anger and helplessness churned in his gut. "He had time to get ahead of me. He could have been deeper in the woods when you saw him, and by the time I got over there, he was gone."

"What about you, Royce?" Dylan asked.

Royce shrugged. "I don't know. It's dense undergrowth over there. Evan and I were like rats in a maze chasing the scent of cheese."

"Just the scent?" Amanda asked this question, the fear turning to self-doubt as her pretty face flushed with bright color.

"Amanda…" Evan stepped closer, closing a hand over her shoulder as she trembled.

She lifted her tear-washed green gaze. "I was sure…so sure…"

"I don't doubt you, Amanda. I believe you saw him. I believe he was here." He wasn't trying to soothe her, he really didn't doubt her. "This is exactly what Weering's trying to do. Scare you, make you doubt yourself."

Break her. And she was already too fragile from her first encounter with the madman. Would she survive another?

The cold early-spring breeze flirted with the short tresses of her hair, lifting the scent of peaches and cream to his nostrils as he dragged in a quick breath. He'd just found her after six years. He couldn't lose her again. Not until he chose to let her go.

Over her head he glared at his brother-in-law, the sheriff. Usually he loved to razz this man, but his sense of humor had left him that day in River City when he had found out what had happened to his missing wife.

"Dylan, you've got to get on this. Royce, have you found out anything?"

"I sent Murphy to town and it probably gave that bastard Weering an opportunity to sneak over here when I did, but he's checking around, too."

Dylan grumbled, "I have good deputies."

Evan managed a short chuckle. "Maybe we should put Lindsey on it. She could track him down."

His sister's investigative reporting had brought her together with the sheriff, the object of her teenage crush. Her investigation had nearly killed them both and had taken some years off Evan's life, as well. And that was before he'd even known how important she would become to him.

Evan's chuckle turned to a groan. "You haven't told her, have you?"

Joking—and infant daughter—aside, Lindsey would throw herself into the midst of the danger. Anything in pursuit of a story.

Although wind chapped, Dylan's face paled. "God, no!"

Amanda shuddered. "No, please, don't involve anyone else. I don't want anyone else hurt!"

"You're sure Weering killed this guy in River City?" Dylan asked, ever the lawman.

Evan nodded. "I doubt the investigating officers found any evidence. But I know he did it."

"That's good enough for me. And since you think

he ran those people off the road last night, I've already put an APB out on him. We'll get him, Evan." Dylan squeezed his shoulder.

A tear slid down Amanda's cheek, the wind smearing it across her face. "Don't you all understand? He's too smart. He's going to always be ahead. He was here, ahead of us, Evan. He knew where my son was before I did. He was here! Across the street from my son!"

Evan pulled her trembling body into his arms, holding her close to his chest while he stroked her hair. His fingers slid over the ridge of the scar on the back of her head, and anger and compassion swirled in his chest.

She was on the verge of dropping, exhausted no doubt from their endless night, and from her paleness he imagined she had another migraine. He cursed himself for pushing her too hard last night, for shoving those albums on her in the vain attempt that she would remember.

That she would remember *him.*

"He won't hurt our son, Amanda," Evan reassured her.

Royce spoke softly as he would to one of the frightened children he rescued, "Amanda, Christopher was safe. This place has a top-notch security system. And there's no way in hell that bastard would have gotten him, not under my protection. I swear that to you."

Evan absorbed her trembling as nothing they said calmed her fears. "Amanda, we'll find him. We will."

Her fingers grasped the lapels of his coat as she lifted her head from his chest. "No! I don't want you to find him. I don't want him to do to you what he did to…Snake. I can't stand the thought of him hurting anyone else because of me. But most especially not…'' Her voice trailed off.

Who?

Him?

She never finished her thought as she collapsed in his arms.

Too fragile.

And William Weering was winning.

EVAN BRUSHED A HAND over his hair, not surprised to dislodge a dead leaf that disintegrated on the floor of the hospital corridor, leaving only dust.

Sarah walked up, heels tapping on the linoleum, and held out a paper cup of coffee. A smile tipped up a corner of her mouth. ''Never thought I'd see Evan Quade so disheveled.''

He glanced around her to where Christopher and Jeremy lingered at the vending machine, Christopher's high voice reciting the letters and numbers on the keys. He couldn't let the boy out of his sight. It was killing him that Amanda was. But she was just inside the door at his back, the doctor examining her.

He'd been asked to wait outside, but he was her husband. Even though she didn't remember. Helplessness had him fisting his hands and breathing deep.

''I'm sure she's fine, Evan.'' Sarah had been a nurse, so he wanted to believe her, wanted to believe that she was offering a medical opinion and not just reassuring a nervous friend.

He nodded his agreement. ''Yeah, I'm sure she is.''

And Amanda had recovered fast, opening her eyes

when he'd swung her up in his arms. Murmuring in protest even while she winced with pain.

"Migraines are very debilitating," Sarah continued.

After she'd left him all those years ago, he'd suffered from some headaches brought on by insomnia. But he didn't think they compared to the pain Amanda suffered.

Was her old head injury the cause of her pain? Or the trauma from the way she had been injured? Not only did a medical doctor examine her, but also a psychiatrist who had treated his mother, summoned by Evan.

"You know," Sarah mused, "I didn't think I'd like her very much."

"Who?" Distracted by his thoughts, Evan had no idea what she was talking about.

"Amanda. But that was before I met her, before you and Royce discovered what had happened to her." She shivered. "But even then, she had left you before that happened. And I still harbored some... resentment that she had hurt my friend, you know."

Evan's heart softened at her loyalty. He was blessed with the best damn friends. "Sarah..."

She blinked back a hint of tears. "But then I met Christopher."

He followed her gaze down the hall to his little boy, and his heart softened even more. "He's an amazing kid, isn't he?"

"A good kid," she agreed. "And he wouldn't be so sweet and secure and wouldn't love his mother so much if she wasn't so devoted, if she wasn't such a wonderful mother. She *is* a wonderful mother, Evan.''

Did that make up for all the years he'd not known he had a son? Because, although she'd forgotten her husband after the attack, she'd known she was pregnant before it, and she hadn't told him. She'd left him instead.

But if he had known, would he have been much of a father? With the genes he carried, was that even possible? Except for the attack, maybe Christopher and Amanda had been better off without him.

Maybe it was time he found out what kind of father he'd be. Because now that he knew about Christopher, he didn't think he could let him go as he had originally intended to let Amanda go. He couldn't be that unselfish.

To let Sarah know he appreciated her support, he squeezed her hand as he passed her in the hall. The little boy glanced up at his approach. ''Hi.''

He and Jeremy had taken chairs in the waiting area where they munched on the snacks they'd chosen from the vending machine. Evan crouched down near his son's chair. ''Hi, Christopher. So what did you pick?''

''A6,'' the little boy replied. ''I know my letters and numbers.''

Jeremy chuckled. ''And he read them all to me.''

Pride swelled in Evan's chest. Then he realized he had no right to it. Amanda had raised their child. All he had contributed was DNA, just as his biological father had.

''Well, that's great, little guy,'' he managed to say over the lump of emotion clogging his throat.

Christopher smiled, then glanced toward the door behind which doctors examined his mother. "You're strong. You picked Mommy up and she weighs a lot more than me."

"Your mommy's going to be fine, Christopher." William Weering was *not* going to win.

"I know. She gets bad headaches, but she always gets better. When she comes out, can we go home?" His dark eyes brightened with hope.

Home. Christopher meant a little bungalow in River City. Evan meant an imposing house on the lakeside, something he'd intentionally built with no warmth, no welcome. After Amanda had left, he had wanted to close himself off from the world. But he had found that impossible in Winter Falls, where he'd found his family, not even realizing he had another one only a few hours away.

He wanted his house to be home for Amanda and Christopher. But he doubted that it would ever be. "Not today, little guy."

"I'm going to stay with Jeremy again?" His dark gaze, full of adoration, flickered toward the older boy.

Evan shook his head. "No, I'd like you to come stay with me, at my house. Your mommy stayed there last night."

"Mommy will be there?"

If the doctors released her...

"Evan," Sarah said as she approached them, her heels tapping. "Dr. Snyder would like to speak with you."

Evan caught sight of the tall thin psychiatrist standing outside the door to Amanda's room. He straightened up, brushing a hand over Christopher's soft hair. "I'll be right back."

"Okay." The little boy stared up at him, his bottom lip trembling. "Daddy…"

Evan's heart lurched. He blinked hard, as his hand lingered on the boy's head. His boy's head.

"I didn't know you had a son," the doctor said when Evan joined him.

"Until a few days ago, neither did I. How is she, Doctor?"

The doctor shrugged one shoulder. "Without her full history, I can't say much. Dr. Barnes and I both believe her fainting episodes have been brought on by migraines, and those are either a result of the old concussion or her recent stress."

"And the amnesia?"

"It's real."

"I never doubted that." Not after their initial meeting, not after he'd learned the awful truth of what had happened to her.

"She honestly can't remember anything from before waking up after the attack. Her old life is lost to her."

To them both.

Evan had to ask the question that had been burning in his mind, that had him shoving albums at her, had him kissing her… No, he hadn't kissed her for her memory to return. He had to be honest. He'd kissed her for himself. For his pleasure.

And he burned to kiss her again.

He cleared his throat. "Will her memory ever return, Doctor?"

Again the psychiatrist shrugged. "It's been almost six years, Evan."

"What does that mean?"

From years of treating his mother, he knew whatever a psychiatrist said always meant something. But at least this doctor didn't use psychobabble. He believed in speaking in terms laypeople could understand.

"Either the head injury did so much damage that that part of her memory has been permanently erased."

How hard had the bastard beaten her? He didn't think he could handle knowing that, though.

"Or?"

"Or she's put a block in her mind to prevent any memories of the attack from surfacing. It's a mental defense mechanism."

"But she hasn't just forgotten the attack."

"No, the attack was so brutal, so traumatizing—"

Evan winced.

"Sorry." The doctor sighed at his own insensitivity. "Bottom line is that she doesn't dare remember anything after waking up in the hospital for fear of remembering the attack, too."

Frustration gnawed at Evan. "So if it's mental, she can get over this. You can help her like you did my mother."

Retha Warner lived a normal happy life now, doting on her new granddaughter and her husband. What would his mother think of the grandson she'd not known about? He didn't even have to wonder. Knowing the size of her heart, he didn't doubt she'd love Christopher, too.

"It's been a long time, Evan. Six years. That block could be permanent now."

So his wife might never remember him?

AMANDA LICKED HER LIPS. Her mouth had to be dry from reading Christopher two bedtime stories. One for tonight and one to make up for last night. He had ruled that the phone call didn't count.

Reading had to be what dried out her mouth. It couldn't be the gentle way that Evan tucked their child into the guest-room bed. He pulled the comforter to Christopher's little rounded chin, his deep voice rumbling with emotion as he wished him sweet dreams.

"I like your house," Christopher said.

Her breath had barely returned from the way he'd raced around the imposing structure, clamoring on the stainless-steel steps and running across the catwalk that separated the master bedroom from the guest bed-rooms.

Evan had not built his house with a child in mind. But then, he hadn't known. Why hadn't she told him about her pregnancy before she'd left? Why had she left him?

Watching him now as he stared down at his sleepy son, she couldn't think of a single reason. But then thinking about the past only inspired migraines.

Both the medical doctor and the shrink had rec-ommended that she not force any memories. And that she deal better with her stress. Suppressing it wasn't healthy.

The only way she could deal with it would be when William Weering III was back behind bars where he belonged. She shut her eyes on the image of his hair gleaming in the woods across the street from the house where her son was.

Too close to her son. She glanced across the bed toward the window, where the blinds had been drawn. Could he be out there now?

Evan had assured her that not only would the security firm he'd hired stand guard, but a sheriff's deputy would, as well. They were safe.

For now.

He hadn't said that, but she knew it. She knew that Weering was biding his time, playing out the plan he'd devised those long years in prison. He wasn't going to give up. But she doubted that Evan would, either.

She backed out of the room where Evan knelt at Christopher's side. His deep voice murmured to their son, "I'm glad you like it here…son."

She shivered and turned away, overcome with compassion and remorse. She had kept them apart too many years. She couldn't watch them anymore, so she started across the landing, wincing against the bright, overhead light as the vestiges of her migraine lingered.

The doctor's orders replayed in her mind. "Lie down in a dark room. Migraines make you light sensitive."

Dark room?

The mere thought filled her with the very stress she was supposed to avoid. When a broad hand closed over her shoulder, she jumped, nerves frayed.

"I'm sorry, Amanda. I didn't mean to startle you." Evan had pitched his voice low, he didn't know how soundly his son slept. He didn't know his son. Because of her.

But instead of resenting her, he risked his life to help her.

His hand slid away. "You really should get some rest. The doctor said that exhaustion contributed to your col—"

He'd cut off his comment too late. She knew what he meant and her face burned with embarrassment. "Collapse? Was that what you were going to call it?"

"Amanda…"

She sighed. "I guess you have reason to call it that. I've fainted twice in your arms now."

"You're under a lot of stress right now, Amanda. And with your old injury…you're fragile."

Fragile. Victim. Anger replaced the embarrassment, burning hotter and more intensely. "I'm not fragile!"

"Amanda, you've been through so much…"

God, she was sick of his pity, his compassion. It was then she realized she wanted his plain passion. She wanted him to burn with it.

For her.

Turning her thoughts, she said, "So have you been through so much…since you found me." Maybe since she left. Had he missed her? Was that why he wore her ring close to his heart, or was it to remind him to never trust again?

"I told you that you could trust me, Amanda. Now why don't you go lie down and rest? There's another guest room, or were you going to share with Christopher?"

Boldness lifted her chin, had her meeting his gaze

with an intense look. "I want to share...with you, Evan."

His dark eyes flickered. He cleared his throat before saying, "I can't, Amanda. I can't just hold you like I did last night."

"I don't want you to." She stepped closer, skimming her fingers up his chest to his broad shoulders.

"What are you saying?"

She wrapped her hand around the nape of his neck and rose up on tiptoe, sliding her mouth over his. "Does that answer your question?"

He groaned, his tongue flickering out, giving her a tantalizing taste of his dark passion. "Amanda..."

His hands closed over her shoulders. But instead of pulling her closer, he held her away, his arms rigid. "Amanda, I can't promise you gentle. I'm not a gentle man. I might—"

"Scare me?" Her heart pounded with fear. It wasn't of him but of what she felt for him. A desperate need clawed at her, and she sidled closer to his long lean body, breathing in the aromatic seductive scent of him.

His jaw tightened, a muscle jumping while he asked, "Have you...since the attack?"

She knew what he meant. Heat flashed into her face. "I haven't wanted to be close to anyone since, so no. But it wasn't fear that held me back."

Maybe she remembered she was married but suppressed it as the shrink had hinted. Maybe she had always known she was married. "I don't know what did. Maybe it was only about trust."

And nothing to do with suppressed memories. "I

couldn't trust anyone, couldn't get close to any-one…''

Not until Evan.

''You shouldn't trust me, Amanda. I'm not the man you think I am.''

''You're my husband, Evan.''

And for tonight that was reason enough to want him. She would not explore those deeper, almost for-gotten emotions that drew her to him. Drew her into his arms again and again. But she wanted more than protection or comfort from him this time.

He studied her face for a long moment, perhaps looking for any sign that she had accepted she was his wife. More than that—she had remembered it.

She shook her head, her eyes filling with tears. Why couldn't she remember him with her mind when her body seemed to remember him so well that it burned with wanting him?

His fingers stroked over her cheek, as did his dark gaze. ''You are so beautiful.''

She shook her head again, ignoring the wave of dizziness, another residual of the migraine. ''Not like the woman in those albums.''

None of her was like that woman, not anymore. She was more than forgotten. She was gone.

''No, you're not,'' he agreed too quickly.

She felt a sharp ache, jealous of the woman she had been, the one at whom he had gazed so adoringly throughout their wedding album.

His voice rumbled deep in his chest as he contin-ued, ''In some ways you're more beautiful. Softer.''

More vulnerable. Then she remembered the picture that had captured Mrs. Quade yearning.

She shut her eyes and yearned, too, for what that woman had had. Evan.

Cool lips slid over her closed lids, brushing soft kisses. Broad hands splayed over her back, molding her closer to the taut muscular length of him.

Amanda's arms slid up and around his neck, pulling him down until his mouth found hers. His lips sipped at hers in gentle teasing kisses.

She wanted more. She wanted everything.

Her fingers wrestled with the knot of the tie at his throat. Tailored suit, red tie. Power tie. He didn't need the tie to show what anyone who met him immediately knew. He was a powerful man. And it had nothing to do with how he dressed or what he owned, it was simply who he was.

He was her husband.

She moaned in her throat and knotted her fingers in his silk tie. "Evan…"

"Shh…" He pulled back, and the tie slid from his shirt collar. "Christopher's sleeping."

"Like a rock. He won't hear anything. Evan, I want more. I want you!" But did he want her?

He'd promised to protect her, but he hadn't promised to desire her.

Chapter Nine

He caught her up in his arms, but his eyes weren't filled with the concern he'd displayed earlier when she'd fainted on him yet again. Now his eyes burned with passion.

For her.

Amanda trembled as desire coursed through her, the feeling new and exciting. The tie slid through her suddenly nerveless fingers and snaked over the railing.

"Evan, I can walk." The protest was token as he swung around and headed for the other end of the catwalk. Over the stainless-steel railing, she caught sight of the slate floor and the puddle of red where she'd dropped his tie.

Then he passed through a doorway into a room where the blinds had been pulled and darkness reigned. She didn't tremble with fear.

Desire intensified, weakening her legs, so that she swayed in his arms as he slid her down his body. She felt the bed behind her knees and Evan all along the front of her.

Pressed close against taut muscles, she borrowed

some of his strength and tumbled them both down to the mattress, which bounced beneath their combined weight. A giggle bubbled out of Amanda, surprising her.

So she giggled again. "I thought I'd forgotten how."

He nibbled at her neck, his hot mouth sending shivers down her spine. "To do this?" he asked, his voice even deeper than usual, with passion.

"To laugh."

"I've heard you laugh with Christopher."

"Our son makes me happy."

Evan drew back, levering his weight off her, but his dark gaze stayed steady on her face. "Don't think that I can, Amanda. I can't. You wouldn't have left me if I could."

"Evan, tonight is not about happily ever after. If I had ever believed in it, I stopped when I lost my memory. Tonight's just about this…

She wove her fingers through his hair, soft like their son's. Then she pulled his mouth down to hers, running her tongue over the curve of his lips.

He expelled a ragged breath, and as his control snapped, he took her mouth in a hungry kiss. His tongue slid through her parted lips, tasting, claiming. Then he pulled back again, asking in a tortured groan, "Is it enough, Amanda?"

For an answer, her fingers trailed down to the buttons on his white shirt, sliding them free until the fabric parted and fell from his broad shoulders. The chain dangled free, the diamond ring winking in the faint light filtering in through the blinds.

Again she asked herself why he wore it yet? To remember their love? Or her betrayal?

Hands trembling slightly, she skimmed her palms over the hard planes of his chest, well-toned muscles rippling beneath her caress. "You're more than I could have ever dreamed, Evan."

Something flickered in his dark eyes and she read his thought. *But not enough to remember.* Hoping to kiss away any pain she might have caused him, she pressed her lips against his heart. Soft chest hair tickled her nose as she breathed in his richly seductive scent.

"Amanda…"

One hand caught in her hair, gently tugging her mouth up to his. As he nibbled on her lips, the fingers of his other hand tugged the buttons free on her blouse. Under the gray cotton, he would find tangerine satin. One of her weaknesses.

Breaking away from her kiss, he levered himself up, sighing and running a hand over his face. "I'm sorry, Amanda."

"For what—"

Did he not want her?

He clicked the switch on the lamp and soft light pooled around the bed, washing over them both. "I should have remembered the dark—"

She pressed a finger against his lips. "I'm not scared now, not with you."

But maybe that was foolish. Because with the feelings he inspired in her, she undoubtedly had the most to fear from Evan Quade, her husband.

His mouth moved beneath her fingers, as if he wanted to voice a warning to her. Then he glanced down, his gaze falling onto her parted blouse and the bright-colored satin bra beneath it. He groaned, then his tongue flicked out, lapping at her fingers.

Amanda shivered over the erotic sensation and moaned. "Oh, Evan…"

"This is just the beginning, Amanda."

The beginning.

She had no memory of that. No memory of this man until he'd showed up on her doorstep a few days ago. But her body remembered him as it hummed with anticipation of the pleasure it knew he would give.

And he did.

More long deep kisses. So many she lost count and lost her senses.

The next sensation she knew was the sweet caress of his rough palms across her bare skin. Somehow he'd unclasped the bra and pushed it and the blouse from her shoulders without her being the least bit aware of his movements. She'd been aware of nothing but the teasing entrance and retreat of his tongue as it slid in and out of her parted lips. Tasting, devouring, bringing her to the brink with just his kisses.

But the next movements of his hands caught her attention as his fingers circled her taut nipples, skimming over the trembling curve of her breasts, each pass bringing him ever closer to the centers that ached for his touch. "Please, Evan…"

The rough pads of his thumbs stroked over the area that begged most for his attention. She gasped as pleasure shot from her nipples to the center of her heat that burned for him. Wriggling on the bed, she reached for him, her short nails clawing down the taut curve of his back as he leaned over her.

But he pulled back, his dark eyes glazed with passion as he stared down at her. "Slow. We're taking it slow, Amanda..."

And slowly she burned alive with desire as his tongue followed the lazy stroking motions of his hands on her breasts. Teasing, tasting until the moist length of it flicked over her nipples. She arched up, seeking the heat and pleasure of his mouth as it closed over her quivering flesh, sucking, nipping.

She moaned and thrashed her head from side to side on his silk-covered pillows. Her hands, still under his unbuttoned shirt, traveled down the silkier skin of his back, around his washboard stomach, which rippled beneath her touch, to the buckle of his belt.

"No..." The protest sighed out of his lips against her breasts. "Slow down, Amanda. I don't have much control left. It's been so long..."

A long time since he'd had any woman or just her? Jealousy ripped through her. But *she'd* left *him*. So who had betrayed whom first?

Another woman, his besotted secretary for instance, wouldn't have left. Thinking of another woman touching him, kissing him, freed her from the last of her inhibitions.

The belt buckle broke loose beneath her anxious hands, and the zipper echoed his guttural groan as she released it. Once she'd removed his clothes, her hands closed over him, stroking the strong satiny length of him.

"Amanda, no!" Shuddering as he obviously fought

for control of his desire, he pulled her hands away. "I want to pleasure you first."

The intensity in his gaze had her lying back on the pillows as he tugged her jeans down her suddenly boneless legs. When they hit the floor, his fingers traced the lace edge of her tangerine panties.

She bit her lip as she anticipated his next move. He leaned down, his tongue smoothing over the bitten flesh of her lower lip as his fingers stroked over the satin fabric covering the core of her femininity.

Her legs parted allowing him greater access, and he took advantage, sliding his fingers under that lace edge and combing through her curls. As his tongue slid into her mouth, his fingertip slid into her.

Her hips came off the mattress, pushing hard against his hand. "Evan..." She sighed into his mouth and reached for him again.

But he eluded her, jerking away from her questing hands. His mouth slid down her arching throat, his tongue flicking over the pulse jumping because of his passionate torture. Then he feasted on her breasts again, tongue sliding around her taut nipples, as his fingers slid in and out of her.

She shuddered, losing complete control under his concentrated ministrations. As she panted, passion wracking her, his mouth slid lower, tongue swirling in her navel before he slid lower yet.

He dragged her panties off her legs and replaced his fingers with the stroking length of his tongue. She clasped her hands in his hair, intending to drag him back up. But she grew weak again as pleasure crashed through her.

When she thought she could feel no more, he gave

more. He parted her legs farther and drove himself inside her, the long, hard length of him lifting her to the edge of ecstasy. Again and again he drove into her. She locked her legs around his lean waist and clung tight to his shoulders, her teeth nipping into the satiny smooth sinews as he made love to her.

Body, mind and soul.

She lost them all to him. And more.

When they simultaneously found paradise, crying out their pleasure in unison, she lost her heart, too. But as she slipped off to sleep in his arms, memories teased her, and she suspected she'd lost her heart to him long ago. And now had no hope of ever getting it back.

EVAN NARROWED HIS EYES against the early-morning sunshine slanting through the blinds, but his gaze never wavered from Amanda's beautiful face. The light bathed her delicate features, washing over the curve of her fuller lower lip.

He wanted to kiss her to wakefulness, but he had already reached for her more than once in the night, unable to accept that she wasn't a dream. His wife was really back in his bed…for now.

Because she needed him. But what happened when the threat was gone, when Weering was back behind bars where he belonged? She would leave him again and return to the life she'd made for herself in River City. And knowing what he did about himself, he'd have to let her go. Again.

Last night, remembering her fragility, he had controlled his raging desire for her. He'd managed as much tenderness as he was capable of.

Last night.

But this morning passion smoldered in him, and slow deep breathing fed—instead of extinguished—the fire burning for her.

His wife.

She murmured in her sleep and her brow furrowed, her dark-blond brows knitting in consternation. Fear. Did she fear more than the madman that stalked her? Did she fear the past, too, and what she would remember of her life as Mrs. Evan Quade?

What had made her leave him? Had she loved him at least a fraction of the love that had consumed him for her? That still consumed him.

He suppressed a shuddering sigh. He couldn't lament what would never be, what could never be. After all she'd been through, Amanda definitely deserved more…much more than him. She deserved true happiness. And as he'd told her last night, he couldn't offer her that.

But he could offer her security. All he had to do was track down Weering and eliminate the threat.

Anger caught flame with the passion, and a thirst for vigilante justice hardened his heart. He wanted to hurt the man who had hurt his wife.

But he had to be the better man. He had to control his anger and be satisfied with returning the animal to the cage in which he belonged.

He had to do it before the man hurt anyone else.

On the bedside table, the telephone jangled. Quickly, so as not to awaken Amanda, he grabbed up the receiver. "Quade."

"Evan—"

"Did you find him?" he interrupted his brother-in-law with the most important question.

The sheriff's weary sigh breezed through the connection. At the dawn hour, it was no wonder he'd be tired since he'd probably been working all night. The Winter Falls sheriff would take any threat to his town personally, but Evan knew that the sheriff cared more about this one because this one was against family.

His gaze fell again to Amanda's troubled face. Even her sleep was haunted by this madman.

"I take that to mean you didn't. Did you at least find any sign of him?" Anything to support their supposition that he had followed them to Winter Falls.

"Maybe."

"What? Did you talk to the River City D.A.?"

Yesterday Evan had left word at Sullivan's office, requesting a call back to him or the sheriff's department about William Weering III.

Dylan grunted. "Yeah. He sent a unit around to the address Weering had left with his parole officer. He's MIA."

"No kidding. So what's he doing about it?"

"He issued a warrant."

"It's a little damned late now." But not too late for Amanda. He would keep Amanda safe.

"And it keeps getting worse. Come down to the docks, Evan. I want you to take a look at a body."

Evan shuddered as an image of Weering's last mutilated victim flashed behind his eyes. And then the people twisted and injured with the wreckage of the car Weering had forced off the road. That hadn't been an accident. The madman had shown them what he could have done to them, if he'd wanted, if he hadn't been playing.

Who else had fallen victim to the madman's games? "A body? God, no."

"Yeah. I put an extra deputy on your place. And Royce doubled up the security team you hired. They're really good. She and the boy will be safe."

But that assurance did him little good. The thought of leaving them while this threat lurked against them filled him with guilt and helplessness.

He'd let Amanda leave once, and she'd become a victim of this man then. If only his stubborn pride hadn't stopped him from immediately chasing after her...

"It'll just take an hour, Evan, not much more than that. I need something to link this murder to the one in River City." And to Weering. "Just an hour."

And it had only taken him a couple of days before he'd tossed his pride aside and gone after her, but it had been too late then. Could he take that risk now?

"She'll be safe. Nobody will get past all that security. But you might be able to see something that'll help us catch this bastard before he kills again, Evan."

He sighed and dragged a hand through his hair and over his unshaven jaw. The slight chafing on Amanda's translucent skin was explained now. He'd hurt her. Even though he hadn't meant to, even though he'd been as gentle as possible, it hadn't been enough. He had to track down Weering, so that he could let her go. Before *he* hurt her again.

"Fine. I'll be there in a few." He reached over her

to hang the phone back up and found her deep green eyes open and full of questions.

"You're leaving?"

"Just for an hour or so."

Fear, maybe left over from her troubled dreams, maybe at the thought of him leaving, flashed through her eyes. He didn't want to tell her about the possibility of another victim and see that fear increase. And be responsible for it.

"You'll be fine," he assured her, wishing he could accept that himself. "There's an extra deputy on and twice the manpower from Murphy Security. No one will get near this estate. I promise."

She nodded, then winced.

"Another headache?" Evan asked, concerned. She had needed her rest, and instead he had made love to her most of the night and then awakened her at dawn. "Go back to sleep. It's very early yet."

"Then where are *you* going? The office this early?" Resentment flashed in her eyes now, replacing the fear.

The emotion was one he had seen a lot of from the old Amanda.

She shook her head. "I—I'm sorry I don't know where that came from. Of course you have a business to run, a life…" But still the resentment burned.

He could tell she thought his business was more important to him than she and their son were. She had thought that six years ago, back when he'd been trying to please her but still please his adoptive father by following his example in business. By letting it consume him. But she'd consumed him, too, with her passion.

In the end he'd pleased no one.

She stiffened and drew farther from him across the expansive space of the king-size bed. "I was gone a long time. I understand that you have other obligations, other commitments. After so many years, I can't mean anything to you anymore if I ever had."

"Amanda…"

"Last night I threw myself at you, seeking comfort, seeking release from all this stress. The doctor said I needed to do that, needed to release the stress instead of holding it inside." Her pale skin flushed mottled red with embarrassment.

"So last night you were just carrying out doctor's orders?" Pain flashed through him.

She shrugged, the comforter slipping from one bare shoulder. "That's my excuse. What was yours? You just needed a woman, and I happened to be willing?"

"You're saying I used you?" The pain intensified, blinding him. He curled his hands into fists so he wouldn't reach for her and show her just how much he wanted her. *Only* her. No other woman would have done.

No other woman ever *had*. Not before. And since, he'd never even been tempted to break his marriage vows.

"I can't do this, Amanda." Unwilling to argue with her, he kicked off the covers and strode from the bed. "I have to meet someone."

"We'll be fine without you. We were for most of the last six years," she said to his retreating back.

Just when he had thought she couldn't hurt him anymore…

Her words still rang in his ears, even after he'd

checked in on a sleeping Christopher and slipped quietly down the stairs and out of the house. He nodded to the deputy at the door and then to the security guard at the gate. But he didn't speak. He couldn't—his emotion was choking him.

Nobody could infuriate him like Amanda. Nobody could fill him with as much passion with a look or a word. She made him crazy with loving her.

He had no more than backed out the gate when he stopped for an approaching car. A familiar-looking sedan. Ms. Moore pulled to the side of the road and got out, running up to his window. He waited until she tapped on the glass before lowering it. He didn't have time for business. He had time for nothing but assuring the safety of his son and his wife.

"Ms. Moore, I told you there's nothing that Marshall can't handle about the business."

She tucked a straggly lock of bleached hair behind her ear. "But, Mr. Quade, there is one thing he can't take care of." She pushed a file toward him; he didn't need to ask what it contained. "Your divorce papers. You need to have her sign these so I can return them to your lawyer."

His hands clenched the wheel. "You are way out of line, Ms. Moore. I suggest you leave right now."

Heat flamed in her face. "Mr. Quade, I'm only trying to help you. You know that I—I care about you…" Hope kindled in her brown eyes.

How had he missed her feelings? Was he so self-absorbed that he had never noticed how she'd gotten too attached? "I'm sorry, Ms. Moore. I never gave you any indication—"

"No." She reached through the open window to

lay her hand over his on the steering wheel. "I know, Mr. Quade. You couldn't. You're still a married man, but once she signs these papers…"

"I didn't need her signature to divorce her, Ms. Moore." She'd been gone so long, he could have been a free man years ago. But a divorce decree wouldn't have released him from his commitment to her then or now. He would always love Amanda.

"I don't understand."

He shook his head and lifted her hand from his. "No, you don't and that's my fault. I should have made sure that you did, that you knew that I never had and never would think of you as anything but my secretary."

Hurt tightened her thin face and dampened her eyes. "You love her?"

"That's not any of your business." He paused and said, "I have to leave now."

As he drove away, she watched him. From the corner of his vision he caught the flicker at the blinds inside the house and knew someone else did, too.

ANGER CHURNED IN Amanda's empty stomach. Anger at herself, not Evan. He'd done nothing wrong. She was the guilty one. She was the one who'd used him and not just last night.

Since the day he'd showed up on her doorstep, she had used him for protection and allowed him to put his life at risk to save hers. And now, knowing how much she loved him, she couldn't do that. Not anymore.

She had to leave.

She flipped the blinds closed, the darkness soothing

rather than frightening. She'd seen the secretary's love for her boss and knew it would be as unrequited as her own love for Evan.

Heat flamed in her face, embarrassment over her feelings but more in the way she'd expressed herself. She'd sounded like a spoiled child. Had she been? Was this the real Amanda Quade, the one she'd forgotten? Had she been so insecure that she'd been jealous of her husband's work? Perhaps she hadn't lost the strong woman she'd once been. Perhaps the woman she'd been was so weak that she had easily forgotten her.

And if so, then she could be strong now. Strong enough to leave the man she loved in order to save him.

She crept across the stainless-steel catwalk, which would have been more appropriate in a warehouse, to the room where Christopher slept. His black curls crushed on the pillow, he snuggled deep into the bed, totally relaxed.

Even in his sleep, Evan had not relaxed. She had watched him for a while, looking for any hint of vulnerability. The man had none, or so she had thought until she'd verbally lashed out at him. Then she'd seen the hurt and how deep it ran.

Would he ever forgive her for not telling him about his son? Would he be able to if she left him their son? Christopher would be safer with his father than he'd ever be with her while Weering ran free.

Could she leave them both and survive the pain?

The mere thought of walking away from them filled her with agony, weakening her knees so that she slumped to the bedroom floor. But she had no time for self-pity.

She was the strong Amanda. She could do this. All she needed were a few things and a place to stay.

She regained her feet and rushed back to Evan's bedroom, her gaze falling across the rumpled bed where they'd found pleasure again and again in the night in each other's arms. Her love for him and Christopher would keep her strong, would remind her that she was doing the right thing.

She had to leave before anyone else got hurt.

Because of the early hour, she dialed the number for Mr. Sullivan's cell phone and got voice mail. She left a message with Evan's number, begging that he call her back as soon as possible.

Then she quietly searched the house for the things from her van that Evan had said the security team had unpacked yesterday when he'd taken her to the hospital. In the bedroom across the hall from Christopher, she found her sad assortment of crumpled cardboard boxes and garbage bags. She had no luggage. She'd had nothing to pack after the attack and no place to go.

The only thing that didn't appear bedraggled and pathetic was the garment bag for the last wedding dress she'd altered and should have returned to the bridal shop by now.

Regret sighed out of her. She had worked with this bride, altering the dress to fit more than the young woman's measurements. The girl had wanted something simpler, more elegant than what had been available in the store.

This was more than an altering job. It was a designer dress. And as an image of her own wedding album flashed into her mind, Amanda realized the image she had designed it to fit was her memory.

Suppressed, not erased.

Hope flickered but she extinguished it. Remembering the past would do her no good, just give her more to regret leaving. Again.

And there was another memory. *She had regretted leaving Evan.* Perhaps she'd even been determined to return when Weering had attacked her. When he'd destroyed her life then, as he would now, this time without ever touching her.

With trembling fingers she unzipped the bag, white silk and lace spilling out, caressing her skin, reminding her how it once had when she'd worn it on her wedding day.

On a whim, maybe hoping for confirmation of the memories that teased her subconscious, she tugged off yesterday's clothes that she'd pulled on when Evan had left their bed and she zipped herself into that wedding dress, the square neckline baring some of her shoulders and the upper curve of her breasts—breasts that ached for Evan's touch.

Had that been what she yearned for on her wedding day? Her wedding night and her lover's knowledgeable caress?

Desire burned deep inside her. Even after last night and all the times they'd reached for each other, she wanted him again.

From across the catwalk, the bedroom phone jangled. Careful of the full skirt and trailing train, she rushed to answer it. "Hello?"

"Amanda?"

"Mr. Sullivan."

"Are you all right?"

His concern assured her she had called the right person for help. Still, she would have preferred Evan's, but she couldn't risk his safety anymore. Or Christopher's.

When she had first learned of Weering's release, she hadn't been willing to trust the district attorney's office for protection, not when the safety of her child was at risk, too. But now, to remove him from danger, she was willing to put herself at risk.

"Yes, for now. But I need your help."

"Anything."

His easy acquiescence summoned the memory of Evan's secretary watching him drive away. Despite their age difference, did Mr. Sullivan have more interest in her than a district attorney for a victim?

She hoped not. She had hurt enough people already. "I need a place to stay. A new identity. I need to get lost from Weering and from my husband."

"Has he threatened you, Amanda?"

"Weering, yes, of course. I told you—"

"Your husband, Amanda."

"Of course not. But he's nearly gotten killed over me. And I'm afraid that if I stay here, he will get killed or someone he cares about will. He's a wonderful man, Mr. Sullivan, and his friends are nice people. I can't stay here and have my presence put them all in danger."

"There's an APB out on Weering, Amanda, in Winter Falls and here in River City. We're going to bring him in."

She laughed without any humor and the heavy

dress dragged at her quivering shoulders. "For questioning. You don't have anything to hold him. No eyewitnesses this time. All Evan and I saw was a man in a ski mask and dark clothes. We couldn't identify him. It wouldn't hold up in court."

She might lie to put the animal away, but Evan wouldn't. He was too honorable.

The D.A. sighed. "You know the system too well, Amanda."

"And so does Weering. He knows he's above it or he can buy his way out of it—"

"We can get him this time, Amanda. Your husband's a powerful man—"

"Alive. But dead he'll be just as helpless as I am. I need to get out of here. Can you find me a place to stay?"

"You and Christopher?"

Pain tore at her heart, a mother's heart bleeding for her child. "No, just me."

"Amanda…"

"It's what's best for everyone. He'll be safe with his father. They'll both be safe if I'm gone. Help me. Please."

The D.A. sighed. "I'll see what I can do and call you back."

"Thank you."

She kept the cordless in her hand as she walked back across the catwalk, intending to strip off the wedding gown and return it to the garment bag.

Outside the two-story windows the sun rose higher in the sky, reflecting off the lake below it. On the upper level, she could see above the tops of the trees that lined the hillside as it dropped down to the beach.

The water stretched out endlessly, glittering in the early-morning sun.

As she paused to drink in the awesome sight, the phone jangled against her palm. She lifted it to her ear. "That was fast."

"Not at all, Amanda, in fact it's taken much too long. But I'm close now, so very, very close."

The voice jolted through her, filling her with fear and the phone shook in her hand.

"Remember me, Amanda?"

Chapter Ten

Evan nodded at one of Dylan's deputies and stepped over the police tape at the end of the public dock. "He's been waiting for you," Deputy Jones said, gesturing down to where the sheriff stood near a tied-up fishing vessel.

Royce and the coroner stood near the lawman. "He's only been dead a couple of hours, Sheriff," the medical examiner estimated.

As Evan approached them, he peered over their hunched shoulders to find a body on the dock. A gray-haired man lay on his side in a puddle of thick blood, empty eye sockets gaping back at those who stared at him.

Horror and rage surged through Evan. "It was Weering. No doubt about it."

Royce nodded grimly while Dylan jotted down a couple of notes.

"Who was he?" Evan asked.

Royce shrugged while Dylan answered without looking up, "One of old Sheriff Buck's friends. A retired schoolteacher. Good guy. Probably just in the wrong place at the wrong time."

"He saw Weering."

"Only person who has so far in Winter Falls." Dylan sighed and slapped his pad closed. Then he nodded to the coroner, letting the man take the body away.

"Did you find the murder weapon?" Evan asked.

"Fishing fillet knife was the doc's guess. Gone."

Knives were easy to find, especially in a fishing town. But still, knowing Weering was armed already...

"I've gotta get back to Amanda and Christopher." Fear for their safety made him want to race back to his car and then race it back to the house.

Dylan caught his arm, his grasp firm. "This guy's extremely dangerous, Evan."

Evan shook off his brother-in-law's grip and his concern. "Tell me something I don't know. This isn't his first victim, Dylan."

And neither, probably, was Amanda. "Royce, have you turned up anything to link him to other crimes? Any evidence?"

Royce sighed and ran a hand over his weary face. "I've been working on it, Evan, working with agents I know. We'll turn it up."

But he didn't guarantee that it would be in time. Royce knew better than to make those kinds of promises.

But Evan had promised Amanda that she was safe. Had he lied?

"There's more," Dylan said.

"What?"

"The killer took more than the knife. He took the

boat that the victim has had permission to use. It would usually be docked here.''

''The boat's gone?''

''Yeah, it was Buck's.'' Buck Adams was the retired sheriff of Winter Falls and Dylan's longtime mentor. ''The old friends were meeting here to go fishing.''

''Buck's all right?''

Dylan's sigh was full of relief. ''Yeah, he's fine. He was late, but early enough to find the body. He also found some money, a lot of money, lying on the body. It's already in an evidence bag on its way to the crime lab.''

Evan doubted they'd be able to trace it to Weering. Despite his madness, the killer was too smart to be caught like that. ''So he tried to buy the boat. He thinks everything and everyone's for sale.''

Dylan shook his head. ''He'll find that's not true in Winter Falls, Evan. This is a good town.''

Evan nodded. ''Yeah, but there are always a few who can be bought.'' Alone, Weering was *too* dangerous, but with help…

''Buck didn't have a gun or anything in his boat, did he?'' Evan thought to ask.

''Of course not.''

But Weering didn't use a gun. Shooting a victim wasn't painful enough, not personal or vicious enough. He enjoyed torture. Half his pleasure coming from the mental death of his victim, the other half the physical death.

''You have to find him. I have to get home now!'' Because with the boat, Weering now had water access. If he could get past the gate and the guard at the beach, he could get to Amanda.

Evan prayed he would get home in time.

AMANDA KNEW HIS VOICE and not just from his television interview or from when she had visited him in prison that once or even from the courtroom. She remembered it reaching out to her from the darkness, wrapping around her, as she lay trapped. Scared. Alone. Praying for Evan to save her.

Then the sunshine blinded her, pain lancing through her head, and the memory was blessedly gone.

But still the voice purred in her ear. "Amanda, are you there?"

Silence was her only response.

He chuckled. "Of course, you are. I can see you. You look gorgeous in that wedding gown. Are you wearing that for me? Will you be my bride, Amanda?"

He could see her. Taunting her. Playing with her.

Where the hell was he?

In the house with her? With Christopher?

She whirled around, checking every doorway for someone watching her with one eye, the other scarred and blind.

No, Evan had assured her that she would be safe here. She had seen the guard at the gate. He couldn't be inside.

He couldn't.

Weering chuckled again, obviously delighted at scaring her.

She couldn't let him win. She couldn't be his victim again. "I'm already someone's wife," she managed to say.

His laughter evaporated. "But that doesn't count, Amanda. You don't remember him. I took your memory away. You only know what I've let you know."

Control. He wanted it over every aspect of her life. And she had let him think he had it. She had given it to him. But no more.

She gazed over the railing, down the tree-lined hill to the water. Out on the cresting waves a boat bobbed. Was he there? Far enough away to not touch her physically, just mentally?

He had stolen her memory once. She wouldn't let him do it again. "I'm remembering now. I'm remembering everything."

"You lying bitch!"

"No, it's true." She continued, her voice growing stronger. "Yesterday, after seeing you in the woods, I saw another shrink, a good one. He thinks it's just a mental block that I put there. So I can take it away...when I want to, when I'm ready, when I'm strong enough—"

"Shut up!"

"And I'm strong enough now—"

"You're going to be dead soon, Amanda. The dying are never strong. They're weak and helpless. They beg for their lives. You'll beg, Amanda. You'll beg to be my bride, so that I'll let you live just a little longer. Just long enough to consummate our vows, my darling. You'll beg..."

From somewhere she summoned the courage to laugh at him. "I'd rather die."

Then she clicked the phone off, breaking her connection to him. But she still felt his rage at her impudence.

What had she done? Had she enraged him so that he would act too quickly, before she could get away and get Christopher and Evan out of danger?

Her trembling legs carried her to the doorway of the room where Christopher slept soundly, completely oblivious to the danger his mother had just put him in. "I'm sorry, baby. So sorry."

For the danger. And for having to leave him. But William Weering had given her no choice. He wouldn't give up and she couldn't risk her loved ones.

She backed from her son's room, closing the door behind herself. At the sound of a footstep on the stairwell, she whirled around, still clad in the bulky wedding gown.

What if he hadn't been on the boat?

How close had he been? Inside?

Desperate for a weapon she glanced around, grabbing up a heavy steel sculpture from the hall table. With it raised above her head, she approached the stairwell.

But instead of pale blond hair, the person climbing the steps had black. Not short like Evan's and Christopher's, but just as shiny. The woman, catching sight of Amanda's attack posture, staggered back against the railing. "Hey, take it easy!"

Dark eyes widened in an alabaster complexion as the woman drank in Amanda's whole bizarre appearance. Simultaneously, Amanda realized who the stranger was.

The wedding gown and the weapon were not the attire Amanda would have chosen for her first meeting with her sister-in-law. Because of her resemblance to Evan, Amanda had no doubt that this was Evan's sister, but a memory teased her subconscious. She had assumed Evan was an only child. But yesterday this woman's husband and Evan had talked about her, Lindsey.

Amanda lowered the sculpture, her arms trembling with leftover adrenaline from her verbal run-in with Weering. "I'm sorry. I thought you were…someone else."

"Evan?" The woman's tone was sharp, her dark eyes full of suspicion.

Amanda gasped. "Oh, no. I wouldn't hurt him."

Liar.

She cursed herself for hurting him just that morning with her resentful words and her absurd accusations. "You must be Lindsey, his sister, right? And I'm his wife." *His wife.* She was surprised by how naturally the words rolled off her lips.

"So you've remembered?" The suspicion didn't leave the dark eyes that burned with resentment, also.

Amanda sighed. "Not really, but I believe him. He showed me things."

Under the other woman's intense scrutiny, Amanda's face flamed and she rushed to clarify, "Our marriage license. Our wedding albums."

"So that explains the dress. Thought you'd try it on to jog your memory."

"No, I made this…for someone else."

"I've seen those albums, too. It looks like the one you wore." Lindsey noticed.

"That's what I thought, too. That's why I put it on. But I really need to take it off now and pack it away. I didn't intend to keep it on, but the phone rang…''

Lindsey stepped closer.

She shuddered. ''*He* called.''

''He? Him? That guy who attacked you and that the stupid politicians released?'' Rage replaced the suspicion. ''But how? Evan's number is unlisted.''

''Unlisted?''

''Yeah, you see how he values his privacy, how he wants to keep people out. This house is a fortress. So since his number is unlisted, how the hell—''

''Money. Power.'' Dread rolled through Amanda's stomach. ''He can find a way. He'll always find a way to get to me.''

That was why she had to leave. To protect those she loved and that Evan loved. Their safety was much more important than hers.

''He can't get to you now. Not with Evan standing in the way,'' Lindsey said. Then fear flashed in those dark eyes. Evan's sister had come to the same conclusion that Amanda had. If she stayed, he would get hurt.

''I—I need to change—'' Amanda started.

''And I need to call my husband.''

''The sheriff. I met him. I truly appreciate all he and your friends, Royce and Sarah and Jeremy, have done for my son and me.''

Lindsey reached out, her hand squeezing Amanda's fingers before she took the sculpture from her. ''I've just learned what's going on, Amanda, but I want to do what I can to help, too.''

As Amanda had feared, everybody Evan cared

about was willing to put himself or herself in danger for her. She had to leave as soon as possible.

"After I call him I'll put some coffee on. I could use some and you probably could, too." As Lindsey descended the stairs, she grumbled about people trying to keep her in the dark.

After stripping off the dress and finding some clean jeans and a bulky sweater to throw on, Amanda hurried downstairs, following the scent of coffee and the low hum of hushed voices. In the kitchen she found Lindsey filling cups and holding court over the men present. Unobserved, she blatantly eavesdropped on their conversation.

Evan, standing taller and darker than the sheriff and the ex-FBI agent, dragged a hand through his hair. "She didn't faint? She must have been so scared."

She could hear him mentally cursing himself for leaving. And since he had returned with law enforcement, she doubted that his reason for doing so had had anything to do with his "business." He had been doing something for her, to help her, as he had since she had first opened the door to him a few short days ago.

Lindsey laughed. "You act like she's fragile or something. She was brandishing that ugly steel sculpture thing when I walked in—could have scrambled my brains with it."

Evan's mouth quirked into a brief grin. "If a bomb didn't do it, I doubt that would have. And you wouldn't know good art even if it did hit you over the head."

His sister jabbed an elbow in his ribs. "I know what I like."

Ashamed of herself for listening, Amanda cleared her throat. "Hello."

Evan separated from his friends at the counter to drag Amanda into his arms. "Are you all right?"

She nodded. "Fine. It was only a call."

"On an unlisted line," Lindsey reminded her.

"There are ways to get unlisted numbers," Royce admitted, sipping from his coffee mug. "Get me a couple more cups, Lindsey. I'll bring 'em out to the Murphys and get details on what they saw."

"They saw him?" Amanda's heart lurched at the thought of his being so close.

Evan leaned back, staring into her eyes with calm assurance. Why did she feel it was only a front to protect her? She pulled from his arms.

"He was on a boat some distance from the beach," Evan assured her.

"He must have had binoculars, though. He knew what I was wearing." She shuddered again, remembering the fear his words had sent coursing through her. And he'd still been too damn close to those she loved.

"By the time security called it in, he'd fired up the motor and taken off. We've alerted the coast guard to watch for him. We'll find him, Amanda."

She nodded although she didn't believe they would, at least not in time. "What else did you find this morning?"

The others turned away, busying themselves with carrying coffee out to the guards and deputies, leaving Amanda alone with Evan.

"They don't want to tell me," she surmised from their fast retreat.

"Neither do I, Amanda."

"But you promised you wouldn't lie to me, and I need to know."

He rubbed a hand over the dark shadow on his unshaven jaw, the clenched muscles tightening. "First off, you have to believe that none of this is your fault. Not what happened to Snake, not the accident—"

"He killed again? Who?"

"A retired schoolteacher who refused to sell him that boat early this morning."

"And he killed him?" She caught the shadow of horror haunting Evan's dark eyes. "He killed him as gruesomely as he killed Snake. That's why the sheriff wanted you there, to identify the murderer by identifying the method of murder."

"Amanda—"

"No, Evan, you don't have to shield me from the truth. I'm not as fragile as you think." She remembered the way she'd talked to Weering, the way she'd laughed at his threats. "I'm not as fragile as *I* think."

And she was counting on that to help her stay away from those she loved.

He trailed a finger over her cheek where she didn't even know she had shed a tear until it glistened on his knuckle. Tears for another victim.

"We'll find him, Amanda. We'll keep you safe."

His hand dropped back to his side, then he turned to follow the others outside, probably to interrogate the security guards and deputies. Lindsey passed him as she came back in, and her punch on his shoulder was full of affection.

"I owe you," the other woman said as she strode toward the coffeepot.

"It's fine. I'm supposed to limit my caffeine."

"What? Oh, the migraines. Sarah told me about them when I dropped my daughter at their house."

"You have a daughter?" Evan had a niece.

Lindsey's lips lifted in an enormous smile. "A gorgeous baby girl. Handful despite her name. Serena."

"That's beautiful. I don't know why I chose Christopher, but the name was one of the few in my head."

"You didn't look at Evan's name on that marriage license he showed you? That's his middle name."

Pain flashed in Amanda's temple. Being in Winter Falls with her husband had just about destroyed that protective block she'd built in her mind. When it was gone, what other memories would tumble back? More memories of the attack?

"But while I owe you some coffee—" Lindsey lifted the empty pot "—that's not what I was talking about."

Curious, Amanda settled onto a stool at the counter. "Then what?"

"I owe you because before you left him—"

Amanda winced, wishing she could change the past, wishing she didn't have to leave him again.

"—you told Evan to find his family. If he hadn't searched for his biological parents, he never would have found me."

Then the woman snorted. "I hope I'm enough to make up for the rest."

"The rest? I don't understand. I really don't remember…"

"Much. You do remember some things, Amanda. You know that Evan's a good man. A man you can trust. Remember that."

How much did this woman see? Had she guessed Amanda's plan to leave?

Lindsey sighed. ''I probably shouldn't do this. He should tell you himself, but he won't. Just like he didn't tell me about the threats against you, about that man on the loose. I pried that out of my husband.''

A look of annoyance crossed the woman's features. ''So I almost died having Serena, I'm not fragile.''

The very idea of this feisty woman being anything but strong had Amanda laughing. ''I'm sorry. It's just that you're the last person I'd consider fragile.''

''Same here. You're strong. Hell, you blinded the guy. And I heard the end of that phone conversation. You laughed at him. That took a lot of guts.''

''Or stupidity.''

''My husband will want a word-for-word account of what was said—''

Looking to change the subject, Amanda interrupted. ''Christopher will be up soon.'' She'd checked on him again before she'd come downstairs and he'd been smiling in his sleep. She hadn't had the heart to wake him.

''Let me make this quick, then, and I'll watch him when he wakes up. And don't worry, I'm good with kids. Who'd have thought I'd be a good mother?''

Amanda shook her head.

''My mother wasn't. She was a mess. She's Evan's mother, too.''

''The rest?''

''It gets worse. We never knew for sure why she was so messed up. She'd been raped as a teenager, and her parents had forced her to give that baby up for adoption.''

Tears burned in Amanda's eyes for the raped woman's pain and sacrifice. "Evan?"

Lindsey nodded. "He just found out a while ago and it's eating him alive. He thinks he's defective now. Doesn't help that when you took off, he got no support from his adoptive parents. They actually believed he might have harmed you, maybe even killed you. Crazy. Anyway, the police even looked at him like he was an abusive husband who had done away with his wife."

Guilt tore at Amanda. "I'm so sorry. I don't remember much, like you said. But I know he never physically harmed me."

"And emotionally we all get hurt. It's a fact of life, Amanda. And we have all hurt others whether we meant to or not. Another fact of life."

"You're saying I hurt him when I left?"

Lindsey nodded. "And I wanted to hate you for it, but I can't."

"Because you feel sorry for me?"

Her sister-in-law snorted. "Hell, no. Because I *don't* feel sorry for you."

They both turned at the sound of little feet padding across the slate floor. Christopher treated them to a sleepy smile. "Hi."

"Oh, there goes my heart again. Lost. Hi, little man!" His aunt crouched near him. "I'm not much of a cook. What do you like for breakfast?"

Amanda would have offered to cook for them all, but the front door opened and the men returned. And she knew she had to relate some information and relive a nightmare of a phone call.

As she headed down the hall to meet the guys in

the den, she overhead Christopher requesting cinnamon rolls.

Lindsey snorted. "I can't eat those anymore. How about cereal?"

She wouldn't have to worry when she left Christopher with his father. They would both have a wealth of support. She'd be the one alone. Again.

RAGE POUNDED at Evan's temples. He wanted to hurt Weering for what he had done to Amanda six years ago and for what he was doing now.

Terrorizing her. And Evan had no way to stop him.

Spending the afternoon listening to her repeat every word that sick bastard had said to her had him torn between wanting to take her into his arms and never letting her go, and never touching her again because he feared he might hurt her, too.

Even now, hours later, he still felt split in two. But he had to control these feelings, had to put on a calm reassuring face for his wife and son.

He played with Christopher. But even as his heart swelled with joy and pride in his smart loving son, anger churned in him. Not for all the years he'd missed, but at the man who had stolen them.

Amanda would have told him about his son. If she had remembered him. He knew that.

Through the fogged glass of his bathroom mirror he stared at his own reflection, wondering how he would feel if he were Amanda and couldn't recognize his own face. Didn't know who he was.

Scared. Lost.

But she'd gone on. She'd forged a life for herself

and her child. No, she wasn't fragile as he'd thought. She was far stronger than the woman he'd married.

A small hand streaked the steam on the mirror and a little face, so like his, leaned close, refogging the cleared area. "I think I need to shave, too," Christopher said, solemnly.

"You think, huh?" Evan asked, raising an eyebrow at this serious statement.

"Yeah." Chubby fingers slid over his chin, still round with baby fat. "I'm getting a beard."

"You are? So that's what that is." Amusement teased Evan, luring him from the dark anger that had gripped him. His fingers trailed along the path the chubby ones had taken, smearing shaving cream along the baby-soft skin.

Then, after emptying the blades from his razor, he passed it to his son. "You better get rid of that stubble."

Christopher solemnly nodded. "Yup."

A muffled giggle tinkled behind him, and Evan lifted his gaze to the mirror, catching sight of the woman who had haunted him the last six years, and who had consumed him since he'd met her.

The last vestiges of the anger, still smoldering, turned to passion.

Need. He needed her. Needed to make love to her and assure himself that she was alive, that she was strong. Last night he'd held himself back. He'd controlled his baser urges and managed gentleness.

Tonight he was incapable of any tender emotions. He wanted to ravage. So he had to keep his distance.

For both their sakes.

But she stopped hovering near the doorjamb and

edged closer, stepping between him and his son to swipe a finger along Christopher's foamy chin. "Smooth shave."

"Daddy taught me. Feel his face."

Evan swallowed hard as his gaze met Amanda's in the mirror. Her green eyes darkened as her pupils dilated, and he caught the quick little gasp of her breath.

"He's hard but smooth," Christopher added.

Amanda's lips curved into a sensuous grin. "Hmm... Is he?"

When she lifted her fingers to his jaw, Evan caught her hand. But then he couldn't deny himself her touch. With their son present it would be safe. To regain control, he guided her hand along his face, his gaze hot on hers in the mirror. When her palm slid across his mouth, he pressed a kiss to the silky flesh.

Despite her heavy sweater and the steam billowing around them, she shivered.

"All done!" Christopher announced.

Amanda jumped, and color rushed into her face. "You brushed your teeth already?"

"Uh-huh." He held out his arms, linking them around her neck as she lifted him down from the bathroom counter.

"You got your jammies kind of wet," Amanda said, taking notice of their son's damp outfit. "Maybe we better change those before you go to bed. I've unpacked all your stuff."

"My books?"

Although her eyes sparkled, her voice was stern when she told him, "Only one story tonight, mister. You had a busy day and you need your rest."

But Evan found them on the second book when he

leaned against the jamb of Christopher's bedroom. She had unpacked his toys, scattering them about the room on shelves and the windowsill, probably to make him feel more at home.

But would this ever be Christopher's home? When Weering was jailed again, wouldn't she want to return to River City and the life she had built there?

And knowing what he did about himself, Evan couldn't stop her. He'd have to let them go. Both of them.

Pain constricted his heart, and he had to drag in a quick breath. They both glanced up.

"You're going to tuck me in again?" Christopher asked, his dark eyes warm with hope. "We're done with the story."

"The second story?"

Amanda giggled and leaned over to kiss Christopher's cheek. "He's a persuasive little guy. I couldn't say no." She nuzzled his neck, causing him to squirm and giggle. "I love you, my baby."

"I'm not a baby. I'm a big boy!" Even though his bottom lip pouted, his eyes shone with love.

"I'm sorry. You *are* a big boy. Just remember that your mother will always love you no matter how big you get!"

When she stood up and passed Evan on her way out, her eyes were damp with unshed tears. He reached out, intending to offer comfort with his touch. But she brushed past him.

"Mommy's sad," Christopher said with a sleepy sigh. "Will you cheer her up?"

Evan doubted he could bring her anything but more

sadness, but he offered his son a reassuring smile. "I'll give it my best try, okay? Now you go to sleep."

He pulled the comforter to the little chin, wiping one last smear of shaving cream from his skin. "Nice shave."

"Daddy?"

His heart jumped with emotion. With love. "Yes, Christopher?"

"I love you."

He gathered the little boy tight in his arms. "I love you, too."

When he finally released him and staggered into the hall, his emotions were raw. And Amanda, standing outside the door, was too close. Too tempting.

Chapter Eleven

He had to kiss her.

Just one kiss.

He stepped toward her and his lips touched hers, tasting the sweetness that was pure Amanda.

Just one more kiss.

A little voice called out through the open bedroom door. "Daddy?"

Evan lifted his head as desire warred with restraint. "Yes, Christopher?" His voice rasped.

"Are you kissing Mommy good-night?"

"Yes, yes, I am."

That was all it could be, no matter how much more he wanted. He'd taken advantage last night. He wouldn't do that again.

"Not good-night," she murmured. "Not yet. We need to talk, Evan."

Her fingers threaded through his, and she tugged him away from their son's room, calling out another good-night to Christopher.

"Amanda, I don't think this is a good idea. You've had a long day, too."

"I need to say some things to you. I owe you an

apology." Her bare feet padded across the catwalk leading to the master bedroom. And he let her lead even though he wanted to toss her over his shoulder and drag her to his bed.

Inside the darkened bedroom, she shut the door at his back. "I'm sorry, Evan. I was terrible this morning. Jealous. Resentful. I had no right to any of that."

He shrugged a bare shoulder, trying to keep things casual even while he fought against the urge to throw her on the bed still rumpled from last night and ravage her. "I should have told you where I was going," he responded, hoping his words hid his thoughts.

"I would have insisted on coming, too." She knew him well enough to know his reasoning. "And you wouldn't have let me. One way or another, I guess we would have fought."

"You didn't need to see the result of that man's violence again." He sighed and dragged a hand over his face. *He* hadn't needed to see it again. "And you didn't need to talk to that monster again, either. I'm sorry I wasn't here, Amanda. I should have refused to leave you."

"You have a life here, a life you built after I left you. A good life. And since you've found me again, I've turned it upside down. I'm so sorry for that."

Why did he get the feeling she was saying goodbye? Dread gnawed at him, and he narrowed his eyes, staring hard at her.

She shivered. "I'm sorry for so many things, Evan. I doubt you'll ever be able to forgive me for keeping your son from you. I wish I knew for sure that I would have told you. I really think I would have."

If Weering hadn't attacked her.

He shrugged. "We had a rocky marriage before you left, Amanda. You traveled with your father, and when you were back, I had obligations at work. And neither of us had very good examples of how marriages were supposed to work. My adoptive parents had a cold unemotional one. And your parents moved from one volatile relationship to the next. We were probably doomed from the start."

She nodded as her lips quirked into a smile. "But we still tried. Were we brave or just stupid?"

He chuckled and honesty moved him to reply, "I think we were just in love."

"I did love you, Evan. I'm sure I did."

"That was a long time ago, Amanda. You were another woman, as you've pointed out." But he loved them both—the woman she'd been then and the one she had become.

She nodded, tears shimmering in her wide eyes. "I understand."

"What?"

"That I've changed, physically as well as mentally." She fingered a strand of her short hair. "I'm not that glamorous woman from your wedding album."

He crossed the few feet that separated them and lifted a hand to her cheek. "I told you last night how beautiful you are."

"Because you felt sorry for me."

He shook his head. "No, I don't feel sorry for you. I'm sorry about what happened to you, yes. I wish I could take it all away—all these years…"

Apart. He wished he could live them again together.

"But you can't. You're a powerful man, Evan Quade, but you can't change the past. No matter how badly you want to."

No matter how badly he wanted her.

He jerked his hand away from her face.

He couldn't have her. Not now.

"Evan, nothing can change the past. I doubt the future is within our control. The only thing we can affect is the present." She reached out, sliding her palms up his bare chest. "Evan…"

He knew he should back away, but he couldn't rein in his desire for this woman. He gave into his urges and crushed her against his taut body, his arms shaking with the effort to remain gentle enough to not hurt her.

"Amanda, I'm not the man you think I am." Not the gentle lover he'd been the night before.

She smiled. "Evan, I know who you are. It's myself that I'd lost."

She rose up on tiptoe and pressed her mouth to his. Her silky lips parted, the tip of her tongue teasing him. He deepened the kiss, but she pulled back and continued speaking.

"But I found myself again, Evan. And I'm stronger now." She rubbed against his bare chest and toyed with the strings of his flannel pajama bottoms. "You don't need to be so gentle with me. I'm not going to break."

Not yet. But he worried that it wouldn't take much.

"Amanda…" If she pushed any further, his control would snap, the very reason he intended to let her go.

"Evan, last night you treated me like I could break

as easily as glass. You made love to me so tenderly. But tonight, tonight is for you.''

Again his heart constricted with the fear that she was saying goodbye. Too soon. When she was in too much danger… It made no sense, so he shook off the crazy notion.

But he couldn't shake off the desire that consumed him. For her.

''Amanda, it's been a long draining day.''

''You're not interested?'' For a moment self-doubt passed through her eyes. But then she tilted her hips against his, and a smile full of feminine power spread across her lips. ''Oh, you're interested.''

A chuckle rumbled out of his chest along with shallow breaths. ''*Too* interested.''

She stepped back, that smile still lifting her lips and sparkling in her wide green eyes. ''You're that interested when I'm wearing this baggy old sweater?''

Her fingers toyed with the frayed hem. ''What if I took it off?'' she offered seductively.

He fisted his hands at his sides, refusing to reach for her. Refusing to help her remove it.

Inch after inch of the satiny skin on her midriff was revealed as her hands lifted the wool. Then a lavender bra flashed into view, lovingly cupping her breasts except for the full curve that spilled over the top.

''Amanda…'' She was driving him crazy.

She yanked the sweater over her head, letting it drop to the floor at her feet. Silky tendrils of dark blond hair stood out in sexy disarray.

She already looked as if she'd rolled around with him in the sheets. Now he wanted to make it a reality.

"Come here." The order was emitted in a guttural groan. He had to have her.

The smile playing around her lips, she shook her head. "No. Not yet."

Then her fingers skimmed down from her throat, over the swell of her breast, across her midriff to the snap at the waistband of her jeans. With one tug, the snap gave and the jeans fell, revealing high-cut panties in lavender satin and shapely silky legs.

He groaned. "Amanda, you're killing me."

She giggled, obviously heady with her power over him. "No, I want to—" She cut herself off, face flushing with bright pink color. "I want to please you, Evan."

Had she been about to say love? While the thought should have worried him, it also, selfishly, pleased him. "Amanda, you're going to push me too hard—"

Her eyes widened, but not with fear. They filled with sexual curiosity. "And what will happen then?"

Snap.

His fingers delved into her hair, holding her head steady while he plundered her mouth, his tongue driving deep into her sweetness. And it wasn't enough. As she gasped for breath, he slid his mouth down the arch of her throat, sucking on the pulse jumping wildly beneath the silken skin.

His hands glided over the smoothness of her bare back, snapped the clasp on her bra and pulled her up, so that he could feast on her freed breasts. With the tip of his tongue, he laved the tip of each straining breast, tasting, flicking, teasing her until she squirmed and moaned in his arms.

"Evan, please, this was supposed to be for you!"

Bridal Reconnaissance

She had no idea the pleasure he found in just holding her. "It is, Amanda. It is." The pleasure he found in giving her pleasure. Mindless pleasure.

While he bent her back over his arm, ravaging her breast with his mouth, his fingers slipped beneath the lace band of her panties. He stroked through her curls with a light teasing touch.

"Evan," she panted his name on shallow rasping breaths. "I can't—"

"Can't stand?" He carried her to the bed, laying her on the sheets already tangled from last night's lovemaking.

"Can't let you do this!" She caught the waistband of his pajamas, dragging them down over his hips and the erection that ached for her.

For her touch.

For the possession of her sweet body.

She slid a fingertip over the end of him, then licked the bead of anticipation from it. He groaned and stiffened his knees as they threatened to shake with need.

Control. He had to find it.

Amanda had all the control now—in her hands, in her sensuous smile—and she knew how to wield it. Her silken palms slid back and forth on the pulsing length of him, bringing him so close to ecstasy. Then her lips replaced her fingers, teasing along his flesh as her soft hair tickled his chest and abdomen.

When her mouth closed over him, he could take no more. He pulled away, fighting the temptation to let her bring him to shuddering ecstasy. He wanted more. He wanted more for her.

His hands, shaking with need, ripped the satin from her hips, and he pulled her up to the possession of his mouth. But he didn't have to ready her. One touch and she exploded on his lips, writhing in his arms and demanding more.

More.

He rolled her over and slid inside her hot body, the pulsing of her muscles stroking him and bathing him in her pleasure as she moved beneath him. Her hips lifted from the bed and she pulled his mouth to her burgeoning breasts.

He licked at the hard points and she exploded again. "Evan! God, Evan, I can't take any more!"

And neither could he. But still he drove into her, again and again, harder and harder. No gentleness. No tenderness. Just raw passion and need. And love.

Love filled him, then he filled her. Crying out his pleasure into the arch of her neck, he felt her sob in his arms and shudder out the last of her ecstasy, trembling in the aftermath.

"Amanda, are you all right? Did I hurt you?" He'd lost his mind with his control. He rolled onto his side, still pressed against her from hip to shoulder.

The smile of feminine power curved her lips again. "I lied."

"What?"

"That was for me, too." Her breasts jiggled against him as she laughed.

And he groaned at the spark of desire that ignited within him again. So soon.

But it had been six long years without Amanda. He would never be able to get enough of her. How would he ever let her go? And his son?

"Amanda, there's something you should know," he said after a moment.

"Baring your soul now? I think I prefer just baring it."

He had to laugh at the resurgence of the old playful Amanda. "I guess you do. But there's something you need to know. Something that will probably affect your wanting to be here."

"Here in your house? Or here in your bed?"

He sighed heavily. "Probably both. I should have been honest with you."

He hadn't wanted to scare her before. He had thought her mind too fragile and her spirit too broken to accept his biological past.

"I thought you didn't lie."

"I didn't. I just didn't tell you something you had a right to know." He rolled away and sat up on the edge of the bed. He couldn't look at her when he told her, didn't want to see the revulsion she would probably feel. "When you left me…"

"When you wanted a child."

He nodded. "You told me to seek out my biological parents, that they were the family I wanted. After you left, I took your advice. I found them."

"I know, Evan."

"You know about Lindsey. You met her and she's wonderful. A pain in the ass sometimes, but wonderful—"

"She told me about your parents, Evan," Amanda interrupted. "She didn't think you would."

He shot a glance over his shoulder, astonished that she had already known. "But you—"

"Still wanted you tonight."

Tonight. Again that qualifier.

"Even though I come from the same kind of man who's stalking you, who hurt you?"

"You didn't hurt me, Evan."

"Not now. But who's to say I won't? That I won't lose control like…he did? That I won't hurt you then? I can't take that chance, Amanda. And you shouldn't take that chance, either. You've been hurt enough already."

Emotion shimmered in her eyes. "We've both been hurt, Evan. Too much."

And now she was going to hurt him again.

AFTER EVAN HAD FALLEN ASLEEP, she took the cordless into the bathroom. As a precaution, she ran water while making her call. After several rings, D.A. Peter Sullivan groggily answered.

"Did you find me a place to stay?"

"Amanda, I was going to call you in the morning—"

"There's no time. I need a place now!" She had to leave before anyone else was hurt any more. She couldn't risk Evan's life to save some bruises to his pride.

But what about his heart? Had she touched his as he'd touched hers? Touched? Hell, he'd stolen it. It was his, more irretrievably lost than her memory had ever been.

"Amanda?"

"I'm sorry." She shook off the regrets. She couldn't let them affect her, not if she wanted to save those she loved. "What did you find?"

"I found you a safe place. I can take you there tomorrow."

"You can be here in the morning?"

"It's a few hours drive, Amanda—"

"Ten. Be here right at ten. I'll get you past the security."

"And your husband?"

"He'll be gone." Her voice had become stronger during the conversation.

"Amanda?"

"What?" she asked at his dumbfounded tone.

"Just checking. You don't sound like yourself."

She suppressed a hysterical giggle. "I'm not. Right now I'm not sure who the hell I am. I just know I'm desperate to get out of here!"

"And Christopher?"

Even though it would kill her, "He's not coming. I can't risk his safety."

"It's a really safe place, Amanda."

She doubted any place was safe from a madman who didn't care who he killed. He'd mutilated a fisherman who had gotten in his way. What would he do to Evan or her son? She couldn't take the chance of finding out.

She let the next laugh, full of cynicism, slip out. "There's no such thing."

Maybe in Evan's strong arms. But what was safe for her was not for him.

"Peter, just be here at ten. Please."

"Of course—"

She cut the connection without listening to him offer what she was sure would have been hearty assurances. Hearty and empty. No one could protect her now but her.

When the night was gone and morning came, she

would be alone. Against Weering. How ironic that she now feared the light instead of the dark.

SLEEP HAD PROVEN impossible. Knowing she was leaving him, she had needed to watch Evan sleep. Had watched every inhale and exhale, and even fingered the ring lying on his chest. She wanted to wear it again.

But it was impossible. She had to leave.

She rose from the bed and walked to where her son slept. Leaning against the doorjamb of Christopher's room, she memorized every detail of his handsome little face. The curve of his rounded chin. The shadow of his thick lashes lying against his cheeks. His hair, so thick and black, like his father's.

He would be fine with Evan.

What she had learned about Evan's genes had no effect on what she thought of him as a man, as a husband, as a father. But would he believe that when she disappeared again? Would he realize that she wouldn't have left Christopher with him if she didn't trust him?

Even without the full return of her memory, she had given him her trust.

But memories had started to return. As she'd lain awake, images had played through her mind. A younger, more carefree Evan, smiling, laughing.

Then more serious, teaching her karate maneuvers and crumpling to the floor to make love. Lots of the images had involved lovemaking.

Overcome with his closeness but needing more, she'd awakened him with kisses and caresses, and in the dark, she'd moved over him, joining them together.

"You're awake early," murmured a deep voice in her ear as firm lips nuzzled her neck.

With a soft sigh, she leaned back into Evan's bare chest. "Yes."

"I'm surprised. I didn't think you slept much last night." His arms wrapped around her waist, deepening their connection. "I don't think *I* slept much last night. You were so…"

She laughed softly. "Needy?"

"…giving. So beautiful. Sweet Amanda…"

"You never called me that before." A certainty born of what she remembered from their past.

"No, but it applies. You're different now."

Not so different that she wasn't about to leave him again. Memories of the first time she had left teased at the edge of her consciousness, but she forced them back. She knew other memories would return with them, memories of the attack. And those memories might prove so debilitating that she wouldn't be able to follow through with her plan.

She gestured to their son. "He's bored."

"He's sleeping. That's usually not that exciting for me, either. Unless *you're* in my bed…" His hand slid up, cupping her breast through the soft flannel of his pajama shirt she had found and donned.

She arched into his touch, wanting more. "Evan… he'll be awake soon."

He groaned. "He will?"

"Yes, and he needs to get out of this house. He needs some fresh air."

"I can take him down to the beach later today."

She shivered. "Too cold. Spring up here is ten degrees colder than River City, and it's even colder next to the water. Isn't there someplace else you two can go? Maybe you can take him to play with Jeremy?"

He sighed. "Jeremy's in school. And what do you mean, the two of us? What about you?"

She forced a yawn as adrenaline hummed in her veins. "I'm tired. You kept me awake the last two nights. I need my rest."

His hand slid away. "I'm sorry, Amanda. You're right. The doctor said—"

She turned in his arms, pressing a finger against his lips, but she couldn't meet his gaze. "Shh…I'm fine. I'm just tired."

"You can rest. Christopher and I can play inside like we did yesterday afternoon."

His concern strengthened her resolve. He was so caring, so generous; he didn't deserve the trouble she'd brought into his life. "No, Evan, this house isn't fit for a child. The railing on the catwalk isn't that safe. And there aren't many toys for him to play—"

"His things?"

"I've unpacked what I brought, which was little. I was in such a hurry to get away. Christopher is already suffering because of my fear. He needs to have a fun day."

"You can come along. We'll up the security."

She shook her head, pushing away the temptation of his offer. "And what? Have Weering try to force us off the road with my son in the car? No. I can't take that risk."

"Okay, we'll go to Royce and Sarah's. Maybe

Royce has some information on those other cases we suspect can be linked to Weering. And Christopher can play with some of Jeremy's old toys.''

He pressed a kiss to her forehead. ''And you can rest. Security will be increased, and the phone's been tapped.''

A few hours later, just before ten, when she kissed them goodbye, she almost lost the strength she'd found in Evan's arms. She'd fought back tears and waved them away.

Nothing had ever been this hard. Sitting in a courtroom listening to what a maniac had done to her had not been a fraction as painful.

But Evan had put himself in the line of danger again and again to protect her, and now it was her turn to protect him.

After watching them drive away, she turned to the deputy posted at the door. ''I'm expecting someone. The D.A. from River City. Mr. Peter Sullivan. Please let him in.''

''Mr. Quade didn't authorize any visitors.''

''Mr. Sullivan is a friend. He's no threat. If you won't let him in, I'll meet him outside.''

''You're not supposed to leave the estate, Mrs. Quade.'' The young man flushed as he made the pronouncement, no doubt expecting an argument.

She had one ready for him. ''Am I under house arrest?''

He swallowed hard. ''It's for your protection.''

''Let Mr. Sullivan in, and we'll discuss my wishes then.'' She closed the door between them, leaning against it as her legs shook. Then she glanced at her cheap watch, hoping the time ran fast. If not, she didn't have long to grab up a bag of necessities and get ready for the D.A. to pick her up and take her away.

Despite the austerity of Evan's house, she believed she could have made it a home for all of them. But William Weering III's release had stolen that future, just as his attack had stolen her past.

All she had was the present, which she would spend imprisoned in a safe house until Weering had been imprisoned and it was safe for her to live again. But she couldn't believe that would be anytime soon.

Even if Evan and his friends found evidence to link Weering to current or past murders, they still had to find him. And a man with his money and connections could hide a long time. Maybe indefinitely.

The intercom near the door buzzed, startling her. With a trembling finger she pressed it down. "Yes?"

"Mrs. Quade, we're letting Mr. Sullivan through the gate now."

"Thank you."

She rushed up the stainless-steel stairs, grabbing up a duffel bag and the garment bag carrying the wedding dress. She needed to get that sent back to the bridal shop in River City for an undoubtedly anxious bride.

As she'd been.

A memory tumbled through her mind. Her wedding day jitters had been extreme. She had worried that as a child of multidivorced parents, she had no hope of a lasting marriage. She had feared that by marrying Evan she would only hurt him—that eventually she'd leave him because that was all she knew.

And she had left him. Once, six years ago. And

again today. She ran from her problems as her parents always had.

Yesterday, she had believed that by leaving, she was showing strength. But maybe she would exhibit more strength by staying, by standing by Evan through good times *and* bad.

As she started back down the steps, squinting against the sunlight pouring in through the two-story windows, she glimpsed a shadow awaiting her.

"Mr. Sullivan—Peter, I really appreciate your coming, but I think I've changed my mind."

The man stepped closer to the stairwell, coming into sharp focus. The hand he rested on the steel railing held a knife, blood dripping from the blade and onto the slate floor. "It's too late now, Amanda. Is that your gown in that bag? Go put it on—it's time to become my bride."

At two steps from the bottom, she was level with his eyes—the one pale and full of madness. The other blind. He closed that eye in a grotesque wink.

A scream ripped from Amanda's throat.

Chapter Twelve

Still screaming, Amanda flung the bulky dress at him and hurled the duffel bag, striking him over the head before she turned on the stairs. She'd gained three steps when strong fingers locked around her ankle, pulling her feet from under her.

Her chin struck steel, but the stars dancing behind her eyelids did not distract her from the danger she was in. With her free leg, she kicked out, connecting once and eliciting a groan.

"You're still a fighter?" He grunted as she kicked again. "I thought you'd lost your spirit with your mind."

Memory. She'd lost her memory.

He was the one who had lost his mind, probably many, many years ago. And now her memories filtered back, memories of engulfing darkness, a trunk lid being raised, her attacking. And she would attack again. She rolled over, reaching out with clawed hands. But before she could strike, the blade of the knife, sticky with blood, pressed against her throat. She stilled as fear coursed through her.

"Stop fighting or this will be over right now, Amanda. And we haven't even had any fun yet."

She swallowed shortly as the knife pressed harder. "The deputy's heard my screams. He'll be in here in a minute with backup."

Unless it was the deputy's blood on the knife Weering wielded. She prayed not. She prayed no one else had been hurt.

He laughed, the maniacal chuckle that haunted her dreams, and wiped away a trail of spittle with the back of his free hand. "The deputy's not coming. Nobody was at the door, Amanda," he taunted. "Evan Quade doesn't have as much control and influence as he thinks. You're lucky I'm making you *my* bride now."

"No." When she shuddered, the knife blade bit into her throat.

"Come now, Amanda. You know you want to. You know you'll beg."

"Mr. Sullivan's here. He drove—"

He laughed again and the madness swam in his pale sighted eye. "Mr. Sullivan can't help you anymore, Amanda. He can't help anyone ever again."

Now she knew whose blood dripped from the knife and stained her skin. Had he mutilated the district attorney the way he had the others—the way he probably intended to mutilate her?

She had to think, had to buy some time…because she knew Evan—past and present—as memories tumbled through her mind. She knew he would come back. She only hoped it wouldn't be too late.

"Why me?" she asked.

"Feeling sorry for yourself, Amanda? So the fight

was just a show? You really are a pitiful victim now. My victim.''

She swallowed hard, resisting the urge to spit in his scarred face. ''Why choose me? We've never met.''

He chortled. ''Not that you'd remember. But no, we've never met.''

''So why? What had I ever done to you?'' Tears burned behind her eyes, maybe with some of that self-pity he'd accused her of feeling.

The laughter dried up, his jaw tightening. ''You were *there*.''

Anger burned away the hint of tears. ''What? I was *there*? Like, 'Why'd you climb the mountain? It was there'?''

He snorted. ''No. That house. You were at that house. Nobody any good ever came out of that house.''

An image flashed through her mind. Removing her wedding ring from her swollen finger while she packed the car. Laying that ring, which Evan now wore on a chain around his neck, on the bathroom counter…of her mother's estate house.

''My mother's house?'' Amanda asked, disbelieving.

''Used to be my parents' house. One of their houses. I spent some of my childhood there, Amanda. But I wasn't a child long. I grew up fast and furious.'' The hand holding the knife shook with suppressed rage. ''Are you a good mother, Amanda?''

Fear of getting sliced deeper stopped her from nodding. ''Yes, I try to be.''

''So you'd never pass your kid around like a party

favor? You'd never abuse him and let him get abused and laugh while it happened?'' A tear slid from his blind eye, over his scarred cheek.

Amanda's heart softened with pity for the child he'd been. ''But then why hurt other people?''

''I would never hurt a child. Maybe Evan Quade knew that. Maybe that's why he allowed others to guard your son, but guarded you personally. Maybe by now he even knows what happened to me. The rich and powerful—they think they're above the law. My parents think they'll never pay for what they did to me, for what they let happen to me.''

''And killing innocent people is making them pay? You're not hurting them. You're hurting people who have done you no harm…'' She forced bile down and softened her voice. ''…William.''

Battling back revulsion, she lifted her hand and covered his over the knife. ''It's terrible what happened to you—''

''Don't pity me! I'm not a victim! Not anymore!'' he snapped.

''So you prey on others, make them your helpless victims? That's only making what they did to you so much worse.''

He shook his head. ''No! They're not helpless. You weren't helpless. Look what you did to me!'' He gestured to his blind eye and the scars on his face. ''You have to pay for that, Amanda, just like they have to pay and pay and pay. Killing them would have been too easy, too quick. They need to suffer the humiliation they made me suffer.'' He turned his focus back to her. ''Now put on your dress. When I saw you in it yesterday, I knew it was for me. Perfect. We have to get married so we can consummate our union.''

Where were the deputies and guards? Had he killed everyone? She fought back tears. He wanted her scared and helpless, as helpless as he had been when, as a child, he had been abused by adults. By people who were supposed to love and protect him.

"I'm so sorry, William, for what they did to you. But killing me isn't going to make them suffer. It's going to make my son suffer. Please…"

He threw back his head, his pale blond hair sliding across his forehead. "I said you'd beg. This is just the beginning, my bride.''

Amanda accepted then that it was too late to reason with him. He was beyond that. She may have lost her memory, but this man had lost his soul.

And how long before she lost hers?

EVAN'S HAND CURLED around the steering wheel as the car rounded a sharp curve on the road between Royce's house and his.

Amanda.

He had to get back before she left with Sullivan.

All morning, while she'd rushed him and Christopher from the house, he had suspected that she had more planned than sleeping. But escape? Why?

Had he pressured her again? Had he asked for too much when he asked for her trust?

After what he'd kept from her, he had no right to expect her to trust him. But if, because of his DNA, she now feared him, why leave their son in his care?

Why leave their son at all? He knew how completely she loved Christopher. Was she leaving to protect him? To protect them both? Was she risking her life for theirs?

If so, she was a helluva lot stronger than he'd realized.

When the deputy had reported her request to let Sullivan through the gates, Evan's suspicions were confirmed. She planned to leave with Sullivan. She wouldn't risk Christopher's safety with the D.A.'s assurances of protection, but she would risk her own.

Did the woman have no idea how important she was to her son? That he needed her? That Evan needed her?

If he was too late, he'd track down Sullivan and the low-rent safe house where he'd stashed her. But if Evan had the means and influence to find her, so would Weering.

The deputy had added more to his report. The guard on the beach had spotted another suspicious boat on the water. Would Weering ever stop taunting her?

Evan resisted the urge to shiver.

He knew the only way Weering would stop. When one of them was dead.

Since the gate at the street was secure, the deputy had gone down to the beach to add extra security there. If Weering thought he could get into the estate by water, he would find himself stopped at gunpoint.

Longing for the rules of the wild west, Evan would have liked giving the order to shoot on sight. Wanted dead or alive. But he suppressed the need for vigilante justice.

They were closer to trapping him. Royce was tracking down leads in the old cases where Sullivan had suspected Weering's involvement. Most of the disappearances had taken place in areas close to where Weering's parents had owned homes. Sadly enough, they had moved often, making the pattern hard to spot.

Evan had noted that one of Weering's previous addresses had been the house Amanda's mother had bought six years ago and subsequently lost in a divorce. The place where Amanda had last been, according to the wedding ring she'd left behind.

Wrong place. Wrong time. And her life had been destroyed because of it. Hell, so had his.

No wonder he wouldn't mind if Weering was shot on sight.

But now was the time to concentrate on Amanda, to stop her from leaving, and to regain her trust.

He downshifted, taking the next curve fast. Almost home. He'd never thought of it as that before...not until Amanda and Christopher had come to stay with him.

The morning sunshine shone off the asphalt and over the bare branches of a tree that had been dropped across the road. To avoid a collision with the thick trunk, Evan wrenched the wheel of the Viper. The squeal of tires could be heard as the powerful sports car spun out of control.

STARING OVER THE STEEL railing of the second-story landing, Amanda sought detachment from her body. Weering had broken her spirit once. She wouldn't let him do it again. She would be no one's victim.

When his fingers brushed over her bare back as he raised the zipper on the wedding gown, she ignored the ripple of goose bumps on her flesh. She couldn't feel revulsion. She couldn't feel anything.

The knife blade pressed to her throat, he leaned close, murmuring in her ear, "I can't wait to lower this zipper again, Amanda, when I make you mine for all eternity."

She suppressed her fear, refusing to feed his madness. He wanted her scared out of her mind. He wanted her to beg for her life. She'd plot for it instead.

Detached, she informed him, "You won't get out of here, William. The estate is a fortress. Mr. Sullivan is the only reason you got in. But you killed him, William, so he can't help you anymore. No one will be able to help you if you hurt me. Evan will kill you."

His deranged chuckle grated on the nerves she could barely contain. "That's what I'm counting on, Amanda. That's what I'm counting on."

"You want to die?"

"All my life."

"Then why haven't you—"

"No one wants to die alone. But until you, I hadn't found the one to share my destiny."

"You've killed others, William. I know you have." She fought against the shudder, the despair that washed over her when she considered the horrible fate of those other women. Those women who hadn't been as fortunate as she had.

"Ah, Amanda, are you upset that you're not my first?" Lips pressed against her hair, near the hard ridge of the scar he had put on the back of her head. "But you're the only one I've felt this way about."

Although she didn't want to know, in order to stall him she had to ask it. "What way do you feel about me, William?"

He laughed as the knife blade bit into her skin again. "You're the only one who hurt me, Amanda. You scarred me. Blinded me."

Would he end it this quick, in a fit of temper and for revenge? She needed more time, time for help to arrive. For Evan to arrive. "I was fighting for my life and the life of my unborn child."

"You fought to protect your child before he was even born. I admire that. I really do."

"You're going to hurt him, if you hurt me."

"He's young. He'll get over it. After a while he won't remember you at all."

Pain lanced through her with the truth of his words. Was Christopher too young to remember her into adulthood if she left him now?

"It's when you're a little older, when things hurt you, that you carry them with you. That you have to make things even."

"Hurting me won't make things even, William. You've hurt so many others, and it's brought you no peace."

"Only death with you at my side, Amanda, will bring me the peace I've been seeking. All those years you had me locked away in prison, I realized that this was how it had to be. You and I…together for eternity."

His free hand gripped her arm, tugging her closer toward the stairs. "It's time to begin our ceremony, Amanda, to seal our fates."

"Where did you seal the others, William?"

"This is about us, not them."

"No, I have to know. You're just going to leave us here like you did Snake and that other poor man at the pier, but the others... No one found them."

"And no one ever will."

"Okay. But what about my car. My suitcases. My identity. Where did you hide all of that? With them?"

He uttered a short sigh. "It doesn't matter."

"I want to know. We're one, you and I." The words nearly gagged her, but she called to mind an image of Christopher, yesterday, riding atop Evan's broad shoulders. She had to be strong for them.

"We're going to be together for eternity, right? I need to know it all, William. Everything."

He laughed again, the sound as soul searing to Amanda as the screams she'd heard from the wreckage of the car Weering had forced off the road on their way to Winter Falls. The sound brought her nothing but despair, an utter sense of helplessness. She couldn't give in to it.

"William, I need to know," she pressed.

"You're stalling, Amanda. We both know it. Don't think you're smarter than me. Nobody's smarter than me. Not even Evan Quade." He chuckled some more, as if he were the only one privy to the punch line of a private joke. "He can't get here, Amanda. He can't help you."

Detachment gone, paralyzing fear assailed Amanda. "You've hurt Evan?" *Please God, no!*

"Not yet. He won't be hurt until he gets here, until he sees what I've done to you. But getting here won't be that easy for him. He's going to be detained."

"How?" She knew Evan, remembered him completely, his passion, his ambition, his unwavering determination. "He won't be stopped."

But neither would Weering.

"Money, Amanda. It's amazing what people will do for money. Keep dirty little secrets. My parents paid out a lot of money over the years to protect my secrets and theirs."

"Not everyone can be bought, William."

"Amanda, dear sweet Amanda."

She shuddered at the endearment coming from his sick lips. She'd loved it when Evan had said it, had wanted to believe he'd meant it.

"Were you always so naive, or is this innocence from losing your mind?" he asked.

Innocent? After what she'd been through, the last thing she possessed was any innocence. She knew how much evil existed in the world, how much bad. But through loving Evan and seeing the loyalty of his friends, she knew good existed, too.

"The man you killed at the dock? He refused your money, didn't he?"

He sighed. "Fool. I wanted to buy his boat. Then when he recognized me from news footage, I wanted to buy his silence. He refused—nobody refuses me, Amanda."

"And Martin Timmer?"

He chortled. "Snake? Killing him was always part of the plan. He was supposed to warn you and leave town."

Evan had been right. William had been trying to send her into a panic, to get her defenses down and send her running. "But he didn't."

"He wanted more money. And I would have paid

him, gladly, if he would have stopped there. But I think old Snake had a conscience. And that's just too much of a liability. So he had to die.''

"Like the others? The other women you killed? How many, William?''

He shrugged, and the blade nicked her throat, the thin scratch burning like a paper cut. "I could give you names, Amanda. But they don't matter. They're gone now.''

"Buried?''

"At sea. I always thought that would be peaceful.''

"At sea?''

"I'm a romantic, Amanda. Your Evan would probably call it what it is—a gravel-pit lake, bottomless due to people's greed for more and more.''

"Where?''

"Does it matter? I can't put you there with the others, with your car and belongings. That had been the plan but you ruined it, Amanda. I had you locked in that trunk for hours, gagged and bound. But you worked your wrists free. When I opened that trunk, you attacked. Clawing, kicking. Smashing your head against the trunk didn't even faze you. Hitting you didn't stop you.''

Instead of anger, his voice rang with pride. "You're the only one strong enough to be my bride, Amanda. The only one strong enough for me to spend eternity with. Now stop stalling. It's time for us to seal our destinies.''

She suppressed a shiver of revulsion. "William…''

"I had thought of having you descend the stairway to me, of how romantic that would be. But I have a feeling you would spoil it, Amanda. I have a feeling you would run if I took this knife away from your neck. Would you do that, my bride?''

She had no compulsion about lying to him. ''No. Of course not.''

''Of course not? You're thinking again that I'm stupid. I'm not stupid, Amanda. And I'm not taking any chances or playing any games anymore.'' He laughed shortly. ''But the games were fun while they lasted, weren't they?''

''Too many people got hurt, William. You're right. You need to stop playing. You need to get help.''

''You're trying to save me now? Did any of those shrinks you saw help you, Amanda? Did they bring back any memories of the life I took from you? They're worthless. They can't save themselves. Nobody saved me when I was a little kid. Nobody can save me now.''

''That's not true.'' She placed her hand over his again, on the knife. ''Evan has experts. People who can help you work through your past.''

''No!'' His free arm slid around her waist, shaking her as he pulled her against him. ''It's time, Amanda. Time to pledge your life to me.''

''I'm not your bride, William. I'm already another man's wife.''

''No!'' His arm tightened around her waist, hurting. ''You're mine now. I pledge my life to you, Amanda, for the little while we have left on this earth. I do. Now you say I do.''

''No, I already said the only vows I intend to ever speak…to Evan.''

He snickered. ''Yeah, you promised to love, honor and forget him. You forgot him, Amanda. You won't ever forget me. Now promise to love, honor and cherish me. Say *I do*."

"Never!"

She flinched as the blade nicked her throat again, this time deeper. Blood trickled over her skin to the neckline of the wedding gown, staining the white fabric bright red.

"Don't make me hurt you now, not before we consummate our union, Amanda."

"I'd rather die!" She tightened her grasp on his hand, digging her fingers into his flesh. But she wouldn't die without a fight. A fight not only for her life, but for a life with her son and Evan.

Chapter Thirteen

Evan pulled up to the gate at the entrance to his estate. His palms, scratched from wrestling with the tree, oozed blood over the leather-wrapped steering wheel.

The deputy at the gate lifted a hand in greeting. "Mr. Quade."

"Is she still here?"

"Yes, Mr. Sullivan drove up to the house some time ago, and nobody's left."

"And the trouble on the beach?"

"Deputy Jones and the Murphys are waiting for the coast guard to check out the boat anchored in the water off the beach, but they haven't arrived."

"But they're on guard?"

The young man nodded. "Yes, if it's Weering, he won't get ashore. Mrs. Quade is safe."

Why did Evan doubt that? Why did fear for her churn in his stomach and dampen his hands, the sweat burning in his cuts. "I'm going up to the house to make sure."

"Do you want me to come along, Mr. Quade?"

Evan glanced around, taking in the surrounding

countryside, the trees barren from the long hard winter. "No, you better stand guard here."

From the smooth cut, Evan had discerned that nature had not dropped the tree across the road. A chain saw had. Someone had intentionally set up a roadblock, trying to keep him away from the estate. Why?

As he edged the dented Viper through the opening gate, he vowed to find out. The nondescript sedan, the one Royce had immediately pegged as a government vehicle, was parked near the front door of his house. The plate numbers matched. This was Mr. Sullivan's car.

Why did anxiety gnaw at Evan? The feeling that something was very wrong, that Amanda was in danger. He couldn't shake the sensation.

He'd had that feeling when she'd left him six years ago, and his frantic search for her had been unsuccessful because of the attack by William Weering III. The attack that had stolen her memory. And again, just recently, he had had the same sensation and with expert help had tracked her down to discover her once again in danger from William Weering III.

Nervous for her safety, he alighted from the Viper, passing close behind Sullivan's car on his way to the door. A bloodied handprint on the trunk drew his attention. The lid was unlatched. And when he stepped closer, he figured out why. Someone had jimmied the lock.

Why?

Careful not to smear the handprint, he threw open the lid. Lying inside was the River City D.A., blood pooling around him from a wound in his chest. Evan checked the pulse in the man's neck. Faint. But life.

Weering hadn't taken the time to torture him like he'd tortured his other victims. Maybe because he feared the guards discovering him. Or maybe because he intended to use his time for torturing someone else.

Sullivan had a chance. If Evan got him help right away. But first he had to help Amanda. If he wasn't too late.

Somehow Weering had gotten into the D.A.'s trunk and through the gate. And inside the house.

Evan didn't hesitate, he ran for the front door, slamming hard into the solid wood when the lock held. Hands shaking with adrenaline and fear, he punched in the code and threw open the door.

"Amanda!"

A scream testified she was still alive. But the sheer terror in her voice shook him to his soul. Feet pounding on the slate floor, he rushed down the hall and rounded the bottom of the steps.

At the top of the metal staircase, Amanda wrestled with a killer. Her kicks were trapped beneath the heavy skirt of a wedding gown, and blood trickled from her neck down over the bodice, staining it red. Her hands clutched at the killer's fists, keeping the blade of the knife from slicing her throat any deeper.

"Let her go, Weering!" Evan shouted as he charged up the stairs, the metal rattling beneath the hammering of his footfalls.

"Stay back, Quade. She's not yours. She forgot you. She's mine now. My bride."

"No!" The denial tore from Amanda's lips, and following some old moves Evan had taught her, she rammed her elbow into her captor's stomach.

While Weering let out a surprised grunt of pain,

Evan moved in, clamping his fingers over the hand at Amanda's throat. He pried it loose enough that she squeezed free, the knife blade glancing off, scratching her porcelain skin.

She stumbled, tripped over the skirt of the wedding gown and fell down on her knees.

"Go, Amanda, get up! Get help!" Evan shouted at her, longing to reach out and lift her up, but now he wrestled with the killer.

Weering regained his strength, twisting the knife and pointing it toward Evan's chest. If Weering had killed Amanda, he wouldn't have needed the weapon to pierce Evan's heart. Her death would have destroyed him.

And now, locked in mortal combat with the madman, he knew he had to win. If he didn't, Weering would finish the sick game he had begun with Amanda. He would torture then kill her. Evan had failed to protect her six years ago. He couldn't fail her now.

Weering's sighted eye gleamed with madness and frustration. "You messed up everything! You've destroyed Amanda's destiny, and she's mine."

No, she was Evan's. But he wasn't about to argue. Instead he focused on overpowering the killer, seeking inner calm while he calculated how to disarm Weering.

From beside him, Amanda moved toward the stairs. "I'll get help. I'll get help."

Tripping and stumbling, she half ran, half slid down the metal steps. "Evan..."

He wanted to shout out to her. Wanted to proclaim his love. But he couldn't spare a minute of attention from the battle. The knife blade gleamed with blood, probably some of Sullivan's and some of Amanda's.

Weering had hurt her again, had tormented and terrified her. And this time she would remember every minute of it.

Keeping his grip steady on Weering's hand that held the knife, Evan lunged forward, slamming him back against the steel railing of the second-floor landing.

"No!" Weering cried out, tears gleaming in his pale eye. "You can't ruin it! I have to have her!"

The tip of the knife pierced the leather jacket Evan wore, tearing the material right over his heart. Insanity gave Weering superhuman strength.

But Evan knew what would beat insanity. His love for Amanda. It was far more powerful, and as he'd discovered, he had no control over it. So he let his control go.

AMANDA BURST THROUGH the door ahead of the deputy. Her screams had called him from the gate, but she hadn't waited for him. She'd run back into the house, desperate to help her husband deal with the killer she'd brought into his home and into his life.

At the top of the landing the two grappled, the knife blade flashing in the sun pouring through the skylights and the two-story windows. She wanted to call out, but she'd done that once and nearly fatally distracted Evan.

Her love for him burned in her heart, the declaration in her throat. But she couldn't utter it. Behind her she heard footsteps on the asphalt as the deputy neared the open door. He'd have a gun. He'd help

Evan while she was helpless to do anything but watch.

And as she looked on, the battle grew fiercer. Grunts emanated from each man as they struggled. Then the blade flashed and blows landed. And over the steel railing, a body tumbled down to the ungiving surface of the slate floor.

Just a few feet from where she stood lay William Weering III. And as his last breath sighed out of him, his blind eye closed in a wink.

She shuddered, wishing for the comfort of Evan's arms. Tearing her gaze from the horror of Weering's dead body, she glanced up to where Evan leaned over the railing. His jacket was torn, blood smeared over it and his face and hands.

"Are you hurt?" she asked, heading up the stairs as the deputy ran in behind her.

The deputy knelt beside Weering's body, checking for a pulse. "He's dead, Mr. Quade."

Evan emitted a ragged sigh. "I know. There's also another man down—the D.A. He's in the trunk of his car."

"I called it in. I'll go see if I can help him…"

Amanda turned back to Evan as the deputy rushed off again. "Mr. Sullivan's still alive?"

"Maybe. He's hurt bad."

She reached the top of the stairs, but more than a few feet of landing separated them. There was betrayal. She'd lied to him. She'd tried to leave again. She hadn't trusted him to stop Weering. She could feel Evan's pain and she wanted to soothe it. "Are you hurt?"

He shook his head. "Not much."

Blood oozed from his palms and from a scratch on his clenched jaw, betraying the lightness of his statement.

He held out one of those scraped hands, sliding it along her neck. "You're hurt, Amanda. I'm sorry. I'm sorry I didn't get here in time. I'm sorry he got to you. I promised you he wouldn't—"

She pressed her fingers against his lips. "You kept your promises, Evan. I'm the one who lied, who tried to leave. Again."

And just like last time, she'd been wrong to even consider it.

His dark eyes burned with concern and regret, and she sensed a wall between them. If he didn't feel betrayal, what did he feel? Love?

He had loved her six years ago. She'd known it even as she'd left him. But her parents had nurtured twenty-four years of insecurity and cynicism. She'd been taught that marriages don't last. The first warning sign of the end had been forecast as a request for children.

So when Evan had wanted to start a family, she'd panicked, hearing the repeat of all those warnings crashing over her. And as her parents had taught her, she ran whenever anything got complicated.

Gave up.

But while at her mother's house, she'd discovered she was pregnant. And she had realized she'd had something worth fighting for—Evan's love and Evan's child.

But did she *still* have his love?

"You need to have that looked at." He slid his

thumb below the shallow cut, smoothing over her skin.

In the distance sirens wailed, announcing the approach of ambulances and other police officers.

"I'm fine." Or she would be…if she could regain his trust and his love.

AMANDA RELIVED THAT moment, bursting back inside the house while two men tussled at the top of the stairs. But this time, when the body bounced off the slate floor near her feet, it was Evan's. It was Evan's dark eyes that stared vacantly at her.

She shot upright in bed, a scream tearing from her throat. Then she reached for him, trying to assure herself that it was all a bad dream. But her fingers slid across the silk sheets. He wasn't there.

She was alone.

The bedroom door creaked open, and she turned expectantly, hoping he was back.

"Hi," Lindsey Warner-Matthews said, her dark eyes full of concern. "I heard you scream. Are you all right?"

Amanda sighed and flopped back against the pillows. "He has you baby-sitting me."

And he'd had the paramedics treat her, had had a doctor prescribe a sedative to relax her. He was treating her as if she were fragile, breakable.

A victim again.

Lindsey laughed. "Technically I'm baby-sitting Christopher. Sarah brought him back to you, remember?"

She'd had a moment's panic when she'd needed to see her son, to close her arms around his small wiggly body and feel his warmth and love. "Yes. I'm so glad she did."

The paramedics had treated her, treated Mr. Sullivan and removed Weering's body, and all the while the madman's words had haunted her. *Anyone could be bought.*

"I kept thinking about what Weering said, what he'd done. And even though Weering was dead, I just needed Christopher here with me, to know he was safe."

"And you couldn't trust anyone else with him."

Amanda considered her words. "That's not it." At least, she didn't *think* it was…

Lindsey sighed. "I can't blame you for being protective. You've been through hell."

Amanda stiffened, her chin lifting with pride. "Don't pity me."

Lindsey smiled. "I won't unless you let the best thing that's ever happened to you slip away because you're scared to trust."

"Evan. My marriage."

"You remember?"

"All of it," she confirmed. "I was so scared back then. It's ironic really. I always thought I lost my courage after the attack. Instead—"

"You'd gotten some with the attack."

"No, before. When I'd decided to return to Evan, to bury my pride and apologize for acting like a fool and fight for our marriage. We would have made it. I'm sure of it. He loved me then."

"He loves you now."

She shook her head. "No, I've hurt him too much.

I killed whatever he felt for me. He holds himself back. He's closed himself off.''

"Because he thinks he's saving you—"

"He did!"

Lindsey shook her head. "Not from Weering. He thinks he's saving you from himself."

Confusion swam in her head with the aftereffects of the sedative, and she fought to clear her mind. "What? Because of what his biological father was? That's ridiculous."

"Yeah, I think so. But there're plenty of people who believe genetics figure strongly into who we are and how we act. Evan's one of those scientific-minded people."

"I don't care what's in his DNA. I care about what's in his heart." And if she could believe that included love for her, she'd fight again for their marriage.

"Ask him."

"He's still gone?" He'd left when the paramedics were treating her, his dark gaze tender on her face before he'd caught himself and turned away.

Lindsey nodded.

"Tell me where to find him." She flung back the covers, uncaring that she wore only her underwear in front of her sister-in-law. She was a woman with a mission.

"Maybe the office. Maybe the police station. I don't know where they all went to powwow." Her dark eyes burned with resentment. "But they damn well better fill me in. I need tomorrow's headlines. It'll look pretty pathetic if the local paper doesn't get the biggest story…"

Lindsey blushed as she trailed off. "Sorry…"

"Where's his office?" She had the van here; all she needed was to know where to go to find her husband.

Lindsey relayed directions with a native's vagueness. But Amanda figured she could stop somewhere and get more information if she got lost.

"And," her sister-in-law added, "it probably is a good idea to go as you are. Might make it harder for him to think scientifically."

Amanda glanced down at her coral bra and panties. A giggle slipped through her lips. "Um…I can always use that idea later. I probably should get dressed first."

EVAN'S OFFICE WASN'T close enough. A little over a half hour later, she rode the elevator to the top floor. She'd driven fast, but thirty minutes was too long to wait to see him again. To plead for their marriage.

William Weering III had been right when he had claimed that she would beg for her life. But Evan would be the one to whom she'd beg.

When the doors slid open, she strode off, determination in her quick step. But she faltered outside his office door. What if he wasn't there? Should she leave a note? Where should she look next?

Inside the office someone moved about. Papers rustled. Fingers tapped on computer keys.

Amanda gathered up her flagging courage and walked inside. "Hello?"

Cynthia Moore, the secretary, lifted her brassy blond head. Her dark eyes, swollen and red, burned with resentment. "He's not here."

She had an open box atop her desk and she filled it with a mug and some picture frames. Her fingers closed around her brass nameplate.

"You're leaving?" Amanda asked, not certain why she cared. She had known at their first brief meeting that this woman was in love with her husband. But then maybe that was why she pitied her now.

Cynthia nodded. "I can't keep working here."

"Because of me?"

"No, you were never a threat."

"What?" Pride replaced the pity. "I'm his wife."

"Not for long." The younger woman laughed at what must have been a confused look on Amanda's face. "Didn't you wonder why he found you now? Why he looked so hard?"

She had. "That's not your business."

"But I know. I know everything about you, Mrs. Quade. But you won't be *Mrs. Quade* much longer."

The woman's fingers, with long talonlike nails, reached for a folder, shoving it toward Amanda. "Here. This is why he wanted to find you."

Although she knew she shouldn't, that it would bring her nothing but pain, Amanda reached for the folder, noting the letterhead of a legal firm.

"He wanted to find you to divorce you."

The folder did contain divorce papers. And knowing what Evan believed about himself, she shouldn't have been surprised. Or hurt. But she couldn't deny the pain that clenched her heart.

"He didn't need to find me. I was gone a long time. He could have divorced me years ago if he'd really wanted to."

The secretary's face flushed with anger. "He would

have realized he loved me if you weren't so pathetic. If he hadn't felt like he needed to take care of you, to save you. He's a good man. He couldn't turn his back on you, not when you were helpless.''

Anger chased away Amanda's pain. She hated feeling like a victim. Anyone's victim. ''I'm not helpless now. And you're still leaving. Why?''

''It's over. What William planned. It failed.''

Alarm shot through Amanda now. ''William?''

The other woman nodded. ''Yes, William. I heard he's dead. And you're alive. His plan failed.''

''You knew him?''

Cynthia laughed. ''We were e-mail buddies. He contacted me some time ago. Minimum-security prisoners have Internet access, you know. But it wouldn't have stopped William even if he hadn't.''

''He would have bought the privileges,'' Amanda concurred. ''Did he buy you?''

Was this one of the people who had been unable to refuse Weering's parents' guilt money? How else had she helped the madman, besides supplying him with information?

Cynthia shook her head. ''He didn't need to buy me. I was happy to help. You'd hurt him, just like you'd hurt Evan when you left him.''

''But you helped him? You supplied him with personal information on Evan, his private phone number, what he had discovered about his biological parents. You betrayed Evan. How could you, when you claim you love him?''

''I do love him! I would never leave him. You don't deserve him! I worried that he would change his mind if he saw you again. I figured you'd manipulate him just like you've done when you came back. Damn Royce Graham for finding you! It was better when you were gone.''

The deranged woman drew a sharp brass letter opener from the holder on her desk. ''So maybe you need to leave him again. As William had planned. Forever.''

EVAN KILLED THE ENGINE on the Viper and drew a hand through his mussed hair. Betrayal by someone close was the most disheartening.

His cell phone pressed to his ear, he waited for someone to answer at his house. Alarm churned in his stomach as it continued to ring.

''Hello.'' Lindsey's breathless voice didn't relieve his anxiety.

''Everything okay?'' Although Weering was dead, he'd learned from the D.A. that it wasn't over. Not yet.

''Yeah, just giving Christopher a piggyback ride. He's a bit heavier than Serena, you know. He's such a big boy he could probably give me one.''

Christopher's giggles rang out, softening Evan's anxious heart. ''Thanks, Lindsey.''

''For what?''

''For being a great aunt. How's Amanda?''

She sighed. ''I guess that means she hasn't found you yet.''

''Found me?'' He had expected she would be resting, exhausted from her horrifying ordeal. ''She's not in bed?''

''Not yet. But I think she was hoping.''

''What?''

"She wanted to talk to you, knock some sense into your hard head."

"She's out looking for me?" His anxiety increased, churning in his stomach as he glanced up at the converted warehouse that housed his office. Beyond the building, Grand Traverse Bay glittered with the reflection of the late-afternoon sun. And closer, parked just a few spaces over, was a familiar-looking beat-up van. He could almost read the painted-over letters of the florist who had owned the van before Amanda.

"Yeah, she—"

"Oh, my God!" He dropped the phone and threw open the door. Amanda had unsuspectingly gone right to Weering's accomplice—the one Evan had learned about from talking to Sullivan. Last time he'd almost been too late. He hoped he wasn't this time.

Mere minutes later when he crashed through his office door, he found the two women together, Amanda's arms locked around Cynthia's and a letter opener lay on the floor.

"She didn't hurt you?" he asked, moving to help Amanda restrain William's accomplice.

Amanda shook her head, and his breath shuddered out in a ragged sigh. But from the wounded look of her wide green eyes, he determined something had hurt her. Then he glanced atop the desk at the divorce papers strewn across the surface.

They didn't speak again, not until the police had come, taken Cynthia away and taken both their statements. Amanda stood near the windows, gazing out over the bay where the brilliant hues of a sunset turned to shadows on the surface of the water. Night was falling. Did she still fear the dark?

"So that's it?" she asked. "It's over."

He nodded, knowing she could see his reflection in the darkening glass. "Pretty much. There was another accomplice on the boat who distracted the guards. And another who cut down the tree to barricade the road to the estate. Cynthia probably found them for Weering. She'll reveal who they are."

Amanda sighed. "Yes, she will. She doesn't care anymore, not now that she can't have you."

He grimaced. "She never did have me. Never would."

"You didn't see her that way."

He hadn't ever seen anyone but Amanda that way, with the eyes of love. But he couldn't tell her that now. He had to be strong enough to let her go, as he had originally intended. She had a life for herself. She would be safe now, safer without him in it.

"So Mr. Sullivan will be all right? At least he wasn't part of it, was he?" A thread of doubt crept into Amanda's voice.

"Yes, he'll heal, but it'll be a while. And no, he had no clue Weering had gotten in the car trunk while he was at the diner, meeting Cynthia. She had claimed to have information to help him. And she had enough information about Weering to entice him to meet her before picking you up."

"She really wanted me out of the way."

He said nothing, hating himself for not seeing that Cynthia's interest in him was obsessive and that she had become dangerous.

"But Cynthia wasn't the only one."

"What?" Evan asked, confused.

"You want me to sign these papers now?"

"Amanda…"

She turned from the window and walked toward the desk. After finding a pen, she held it over the documents. "It's all over now, right? Weering's gone. Cynthia arrested."

"Royce found links between Weering and the disappearances of those other women. And with the information you got him to reveal about the gravel-pit lake, we'll find them. We'll give those families some closure."

"Is that what this is, Evan?" She tapped the pen against the papers. "Closure. You could have divorced me without finding me. You needed to do it for closure? To end our lives together? If that's what you want, I'll sign right now."

He fought the urge to sweep the papers away. After what he'd done, killing Weering, how could she not see that he was dangerous? How could she not want to leave him? "I don't blame you for wanting to sign."

"You think this is what I want?"

"You left me once."

"Because I was young and stupid and at the mercy of pregnancy hormones before I ever knew I was pregnant."

"You remember?" Evan asked.

"Everything. I didn't know I was pregnant when I left. I just jumped to conclusions when you wanted a baby. I thought you thought something was missing from our marriage, that maybe we needed more love in it."

He couldn't let her believe that, no matter what the future held. "That wasn't it. It was because we had so much love that we had plenty to share."

"I realized that later, when I put my insecurities aside and stopped listening to my parents' bad advice. I was coming back to you when Weering grabbed me." Wincing, she squeezed her eyes shut, and he knew she remembered the rest of it. The attack.

He stepped closer, reaching out to her before he caught himself, and his arms dropped back to his sides. He had no comfort to offer her.

She opened her eyes, tears glistening in them. "And today, I realized I shouldn't go. That I shouldn't run away again. But by then, it was too late. Weering had already gotten inside the house."

"I'm sorry, Amanda."

"About what?" Her blond eyebrows knitted together. "If I hadn't lied to you, if I hadn't tried to leave, Weering never would have gotten in."

She snorted derisively. "Ironic, really. I was leaving in order to protect you and Christopher, but I put you in more danger. Every time I close my eyes I see you falling instead of him. It'll haunt me, Evan."

She would haunt him if he let her just walk away again. "I killed him, Amanda. How can you forget that, even for a minute?" He wouldn't be able to, ever. He had killed a man. Now he really knew what he was capable of, and so did she. He couldn't expect her to stay.

"You were fighting for your life. And mine. You had no choice."

"Amanda…"

"It was him or you, Evan. You had to. It has nothing to do with what your biological father was. That man, his DNA, has nothing to do with you, with the good man you are today."

"Amanda, you don't know that."

"And when you think about it, Christopher has those genes, too. Once you found out, you probably never intended to have a child, did you?"

He winced, remembering the pain of his decision.

"I remember everything, Evan. I remember how badly you wanted a child." Her green eyes glittered with unshed tears. "And now you have one. Do you think Christopher is defective because he carries the same genetic material you do?"

"No! Of course not. He's a sweet little boy. Smart and loving…"

"And you're just going to let him go, so you what?—don't contaminate him?"

The way she said it made him sound foolish. Evan was never foolish. "It's not that simple."

"No, it's not. Life isn't simple. We all have things that affect who we are. Things that have happened to us. Lack of love, nurturing."

He knew she remembered what Weering had told her about his childhood. And that she hurt for the child he'd been. Evan did, too. A child needed to be loved.

Now that Christopher knew he had a father, it would hurt him to lose him. And it would hurt Evan more. "I will want to see Christopher, to build a relationship with him."

"And me? Do you want to see me? Or do you want to sever your relationship with me? If you want me to sign these papers, I will. But you better not be letting me go to save me from yourself. The only reason I'll sign these papers is because you don't love me anymore. Because I've broken your trust so many times that you can never love me again.''

The pen shook in her trembling hand. "Do you want me to sign, Evan? Do you want me to leave again?''

He took the pen from her and pitched it over his shoulder. Then he swept the papers from the desk. "No, Amanda. I can't let you leave. Winter Falls is your home now. Surely you feel that it is?''

More tears glistened in her eyes. "Home? I don't know, Evan. I have nothing to compare it to. What makes a home a home?''

"Friends.''

He strode around the desk, coming up hard against her soft yielding body.

She smiled and melted against him. "Sarah. Royce. Jeremy. Yes, I have friends now.''

"Family.''

"Lindsey. Dylan. Your mother that I can't wait to meet. Yes, I have family now.''

And he'd track down her mother and father, bring them back into her life from whatever ends of the world they were in now. If she stayed...

"I know the house needs work.'' He hadn't built it with the idea of having a family but of always living alone.

"I don't know. The sun streams through it so beautifully...''

But would she ever be able to live there without remembering Weering? "I have more land on the

lake. We can build another. We can build a life together, Amanda.''

''We already have a life together, Evan. A son together. And since we never used protection, maybe
another on the way...''

He, who was always so in control, never had it
around her. While once it might have frightened him,
he knew now that he would never hurt her...unless
he let her go.

Hope brightened her eyes, but she waited, fearful
that he might still pull back. He wanted to protect her
from all her fears, and the only way he knew how
was to face his own.

''I love you, Amanda. I have always loved you,
and I always will.''

A sigh slipped through her lips, her breath flutter-
ing against his throat. ''Evan, I love you, too, so
much. Always and forever.''

When he reached for her, she stepped back with a
teasing smile playing over her full lips. ''Not yet, you
have a piece of my jewelry I need back.''

With a teasing smile of his own, he pulled the
necklace from his pocket. ''This?''

The chain slid through her fingers and puddled on
the floor. ''I don't care about my first name. I want
my last back, Evan.''

She attacked the buttons on his shirt, her palms
sliding over his chest as she bared it. ''Hmm...oh
yeah, my ring. Where's my ring?''

He'd taken off the chain, no longer needing to remind himself of anything where Amanda was concerned. He'd already accepted that she hadn't be-

trayed him. And he knew he'd never forget loving her.

He reached inside his other pocket, pulling out the diamond. Despite the darkness descending on them, the ring gleamed like a beacon of light. Of hope.

He lifted her hand from his chest, and as he slid the band onto her finger, he repeated his vows, "With this ring, I thee wed. I promise to love, honor and cherish you until death do us part."

A tear slid down Amanda's cheek as she gazed down at the ring. He hoped happy tears.

"I promise to love, honor and never forget you, Evan. And I hadn't." She pressed a hand to her heart. "Not here. Maybe my mind had hid the memories of you from me, but from the moment I opened my door to you in River City, my heart knew. I had never stopped loving you. The heart never forgets, Evan."

"No." His hadn't ever forgotten, ever stopped loving her, either. "The heart never forgets." It held memories as clearly as the mind, maybe more clearly.

How much of the horror of the last six years would live on with them in haunting memories? But it would only make them remember how very precious their love was. And they would never take their happiness for granted.

They sealed their reunion with a kiss, a brushing of lips against lips and bodies against bodies. Teasing, until passion caught fire, and they consumed each other.

A love like theirs could never be forgotten.

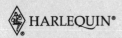

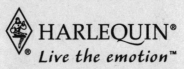

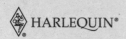

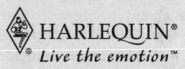

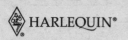 HARLEQUIN®

INTRIGUE

**Silent memories unlock
simmering passions in...**

**A thrilling new theme promotion about the
danger these couples face when they recover lost
memories—and lose their hearts in the process!**

BRIDAL RECONNAISSANCE by Lisa Childs
February 2004

MEMORY RELOAD by Rosemary Heim
March 2004

SUDDEN RECALL by Jean Barrett
April 2004

EMERGENCY CONTACT by Susan Peterson
May 2004

Available at your favorite retail outlet.

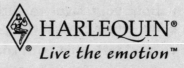

HARLEQUIN®

Live the emotion™

Visit us at www.eHarlequin.com

HIDBMINI

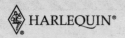

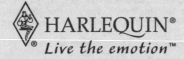